The GREEN HOUSE

DAN LAWTON

Black Rose Writing | Texas

ISBN: 978-1-68433-473-5
PUBLISHED BY BLACK ROSE WRITING
www.blackrosewriting.com

Printed in the United States of America
Suggested Retail Price (SRP) $17.95

The Green House is printed in Calluna

This book is for You—for those who know the battle of trying to support someone who is struggling. This book is also for Me, for the same reasons.

MORE TITLES FROM DAN LAWTON

Plum Springs

Amber Alert

Operation Salazar

Deception

The
GREEN
HOUSE

CHAPTER ONE: Tuesday

Pink was a delicacy. Innocence was its essence, with friendship and virtue being where every relationship began—man and man; man and nature; man and spirit. Without friendship first, love had no room to blossom. Without love, there was no man. And without man, there was no spirit, and no life.

Girard's hand was not as steady as he yearned it to be. There was once a day when he could have reached down with his shears and trimmed the edges of the flower's petals, and it would have been precise. Now, as he did the same, the loops shook around his fingers as if in vibration. He could get closer and use both hands to steady the tool, but he would not. His limitations as an older man had become apparent, and he would not risk causing an imperfection to try to convince himself of who he no longer was. The flowers deserved to live in harmony together.

Through the glass ceiling of the green house, the sun shone and kissed the tip of Girard's nose. He turned his back to the light and checked his wristwatch, watched as the second hand ticked closer to ten o'clock. Four minutes away. Girard stood up straight, let the pain of his years come and go, and started for the living house. He walked the long way around the flowerbeds.

The green house was his oasis. Within its walls encompassed everything that ever mattered to Girard, and all the experiences that came with them—the grief, the regret, the failure, the love. Everything. The walls, both inside and out, were painted green and were harmonious with his life. Being within them brought him to places nowhere else in the natural world could. The green house soothed him, wrapped its tentacles around him and gave him strength and comfort and purpose. The way it made him feel was euphoric, so that was where he spent most of his time—graciously enveloped within its walls.

Girard Remington was a Professor of Mathematics at Carroll College in Helena, Montana, but his career failed to define him. He only taught when he had to, never more. His career meant next to nothing to him, except for the inevitable demands of life that required him to have one. It if were up to him, he would go without. He did not care to talk about it much, so he did not.

And that was that.

The green house was his life.

It, and Miriam.

The temperature was set at precisely 76.4 degrees, never wavering, and the humidity was carefully monitored. The inside was sheltered by exhaustive planning and careful execution and only the finest materials. It was entirely enclosed. No bugs or bees or critters infiltrated, and the purified air could not escape, which created an ideal environment for the flowers to flourish. The windows were covered with forest green plastic that kept unwanted eyes out, but the top was open. Glass panels lined the roof, each slightly pitched so they met in the middle at the peak, which allowed the sky to admire the kaleidoscopic of colors that were beneath. The flowers got the natural rays they needed to grow, and Girard kept his masterpiece to himself.

Whatever troubles arose while in the outside world disappeared when he was within the comforts of the green house. It was the one place on the planet where Girard felt he could be himself. Miriam understood it and accepted it and encouraged it, and she let him have it. She occasionally joined him for a moment of serenity when needed. Not a day passed without Girard showing Miriam how much he appreciated her for that—for her embracement of its importance to him. Actions meant so much more than words ever could, and in their lives, that sentiment could not have been truer. So he expressed his gratitude by reminding her of his love every day in the best way he knew how.

The green house saved Girard's life. When he was at his worst all those years ago, the green house was the one place Girard could go to clear his mind. Still, these days, it was the only place that could keep him sane. Although the term was relative, was it not? Everyone had a bit of insanity hidden inside them. Girard thought so. Or maybe he was reaching, hoping to find some semblance of normalcy in his life, for someone to relate to. Maybe some people hid it or coped with it better than others. Girard loathed his.

Aside from Miriam, the flower gardens were the most important objects in Girard's life. The green house was filled with them. Marble stones were laid in a rectangle around the perimeter of the green house, which created a walkway that would facilitate undisturbed blossoming. Girard paid top dollar for the work, hiring the landscapers with the highest level of workmanship rather than the lowest price. He was not always like that, but there was no such thing, in his mind, as paying too much to assure the gardens would be surrounded by the most pristine conditions possible. There was no price for perfection.

There was something special about the green house, something more than symmetrical flowerbeds with a potpourri of colors, and it was the most meaningful part. The two far corners each had their own smaller gardens, both with a hand-picked unique floral arrangement. The one on the far left had a statue of a frog in the center, the lily pad underneath its feet snaked with veins. The frog's lips were spread and its tongue protruded from its mouth as if it were about to reach for a snack. At the end of its tongue was a hole wide enough to stick a finger inside, and it continuously spat an arc of water into a basin and reused it. Girard kept it connected to electricity, and it was always powered up.

The garden in the other corner was much of the same—filled with a hand-picked arrangement and had a unique water display that always ran. This one was a stone waterfall, and the pool underneath was filled with shiny gemstones and rocks and pebbles that radiated beneath the glasslike surface. Girard cleaned out both spouts—the frog's tongue and the waterfall—once weekly so the water would be unclouded and the algae would remain nonintrusive.

Why?

Because they were Miriam's gardens, and that was the way she liked them.

Girard stopped at the frog garden and dropped to a knee. The stone underneath his leg felt like one, but Girard knew it was a sign his age had inevitably caught up with him. The shears in his hand were rusted around the finger loops from years of overuse, and the knives stuck when he pulled them apart. But they were the best, most precise cutters he ever owned, and they snipped the stems with ease. Today was Tuesday, which meant Miriam would get a pink flower—a rose. Girard leaned in and snipped the stem of the one that was furthest away.

He held the rose to his nose and breathed in. The petals lifted as he inhaled and filled his nostrils with the magnificent floral aroma that was nothing short of sensual. His eyes closed because they had no choice, powerless against the pull of the petals. The back of his neck tingled with rapture. Flowers had a way of overtaking his body, of making him feel weightless and carefree. The problem with that, though, was once the sensation passed and reality set back in, it tossed Girard to the stone as if he were one himself. Then his high would dwindle and he would be back to feeling nothing again—to being numb and empty. But he would always pick himself up off the stone, like now, and check his watch. Then he would walk along the pathway in silence, finger the stem in his hand, and join Miriam for coffee at ten o'clock.

Today was no different than any other day—he experienced the high, felt the crash, and was given a strong dose of reality thereafter. His reality. Miriam would be waiting for him with the coffee already brewed, two mugs steaming, the acrylic watering can full of sugar resting on its saucer in the center of the dining room table they shared for four decades. Girard would present Miriam with her daily flower, and she would kiss him on the cheek and drop it in a vase that had already been cleaned, the previous day's gift already discarded. Today would be no different.

Although, somehow, Girard got the sense that maybe it would, but he did not know how.

CHAPTER TWO

The first sign something was off was the smell. It was not as if Girard smelled decay or hot blood or a smoking gun, because he did not. The scent usually hit his nose before the back door was closed, before he stepped toward the dining room, but not today. He smelled nothing. That had never happened.

Girard wriggled his nose and inhaled sharply, filling his nostrils with chilled air. The clock on the microwave told him he was on time—one minute remained before ten o'clock. He stepped further into the kitchen. Oak cabinets lined the wall as if they were puzzle pieces, each one fitting perfectly with the next, the combination of them forming an L. A green marble countertop sat a few feet underneath them, the tops of which were covered with portable appliances and cooking supplements and a rack of recipe books. The coffee machine was of great interest.

It was in the corner where the two edges of the L met, near the window. The window overlooked the backyard, although much of the grass had been covered up by the green house. Miriam kept a bird feeder stocked full during the warmest months, and it was strategically placed so she could observe it while she washed the dishes after breakfast. A privacy fence blocked out everything else beyond the property line, and that was just the way Girard liked it.

Next to the coffee machine were two mugs, both solid white and so clean they shone. A filter sat idly next to them, also white and made of flimsy paper, not yet filled with the grounds Girard knew he took for granted. The storage container's lid was popped off, the scooper hidden somewhere inside like a buried treasure. Girard moved toward it and looked inside. The scent hit him then, and he closed his eyes.

It was faint, the scent, like the way the house smelled when Miriam baked. Girard could tell when she was up to something, even from inside the green house. He would sometimes get the sense Miriam was busying herself in the kitchen, even if what he got a whiff of was phantom. It was the love he smelled, and that was not something someone could measure. But Girard could—he could tell when Miriam was having a good day. The good days were the best kind. They reminded him of what made the bad ones worth it.

Girard opened his eyes, blinked away the blur. His eyes stung.

Something was wrong.

Even on the bad days, Miriam would always have coffee ready. There were times when they would sit together at the dining room table and be still, only moving to sip from their mugs. Crossword puzzles were reserved for the good days. Words were seldom spoken, but that was every day—even the good ones. Silence was the only way to keep away the memories. Talking made it worse.

While they sipped their coffees, Girard would slip his fingers in between Miriam's and they would hold each other. Their fingers fit so perfectly together it was as if they were made for one another. Girard often wondered how that could happen—how two soulmates could meet and realize their compatibility and be astute enough act upon it at the moment. The world was such a gigantic place that it seemed unlikely, impossible even. The statistical probability of it was staggeringly low. He and Miriam were the lucky ones; most lovers had simply settled, and who could blame them? It was not every day two perfectly connected souls found each other. Timing, while undeniably coincidental, was everything in this life. That was one time Girard did something right.

It was not panic Girard felt—he did not get to experience a wide range of powerful emotions like that anymore—but it was something similar. His heart still reacted to emotions the way it should—it sped up when he was excited or nervous or anxious, and it would slow down when he was content or in deep thought—even if his brain did not. The hammering in his chest made the tremor in his hand worse. He chose not to put the cover over the coffee grounds and took off for the dining room, clutching onto the stem of the rose as if it were a life preserver.

The dining room was empty. The table sat eight, but it rarely ever did more than two. A corner cabinet was at the far end of the room and was filled with the finest china and glassware they owned, each piece delicately organized so it could be seen through the glass front. The bottom was enclosed, the contents inside hidden. Its purpose was obvious—and it was used for it at one time, many years ago—but it had been empty for some time. There was no poison anywhere in the house, not anymore. Even the tumblers were put away, stashed out of sight. Temptation hardly arose these days.

On the table was the same throw that had been there for decades. Outlined rectangles inside of larger ones decorated it, each a different color, each just as bland as the one that surrounded it. The cream-colored backdrop looked white when the chandelier illuminated but was otherwise dull. Miriam loved it. She swapped it only for the month of December, but come January one, back on it went. Girard thought the colors of the holidays were a welcomed change when they came, but he was just as eager to toss them away until the following year as Miriam was. There was not much they disagreed on.

Paintings covered the walls. There was a pastel fruit basket and a watercolor oceanic landscape and an abstract swirl that Girard somedays thought was a sandstorm, while others it could have been the vortex of a tornado, painted from inside the funnel. Miriam chose them all. Girard just hung them. He grew to appreciate even the ones he was not particularly fond of.

At the head of the table was Girard's chair, and the one to the right of it was Miriam's. Except it was not, not today. Where it usually sat no longer did, and Girard felt uneasy. As his hand shook again, he stepped around the corner and peered at the floor, hoping and praying Miriam had not fallen, and saw something else. It was the chair, the one Miriam usually sat in, the one that smelled like her perfume and had a faded seat from the years of daily coffee breaks and mealtimes. It was on its back, having somehow toppled that way.

Girard did not fret. He took a deep breath and felt his heartbeat slow, and he thought realistically about the possibilities. Miriam had not had a medical emergency—that was a good thing, a victory if nothing else. Had she simply had an urgent digestion issue or a disagreement with the imported cod they ate a night earlier? Maybe so. Or maybe not. There was no way to know, and he did not want to speculate. He spent a great deal of time at his job speculating what the next step might be to find a solution to an equation, and he preferred to keep that habitually absent from his daily life.

Girard potted the pink rose in the tiny vase on the table. The acrylic watering can full of sugar sat nearby, offering its company. He crouched down and picked up the chair, pushed it in, and started for the upstairs. The bathroom downstairs was only for guests, although they infrequently had any, so he did not check there. He did not bother calling out for Miriam either, because it would have been pointless if he had. He briskly ascended the stairs as if it were an escalator. His momentum pushed him to the top like he belonged.

Girard checked all the rooms. The bathroom sat idly, the sink dry, the lid of the toilet flat against the seat, the mirror covered. There were not any obvious signs of recent use. Miriam's sewing room was empty too. The wooden rocker was pushed in as it usually was, hovering over a single pedal that attached to the machine with a cord. The curtains were drawn.

In their bedroom, the bed lay undisturbed, the bulky comforter unwrinkled and creased at the pillow line. Girard crossed the room and slid the curtain back, peeked into the driveway below, and saw nothing unusual. A beautiful downy woodpecker chipped away at an aspen across the way, the red patch on its skull as bright as the sun. It stopped as if it felt someone lurking, then jammed its beak back into the hole and began jackhammering away. Girard watched until it paused again.

He retreated downstairs. He checked the bathroom and the living room, then doubled back to the dining room and kitchen for a second time. He opened the door to the basement, saw that the light was off, and closed it again. He stood in the hallway for a beat, paused to think about what he missed.

The garage. He headed there. He and Miriam shared a 2000 Buick Century, golden brown and hassle-free. It was not the most attractive vehicle on the road, but it had fewer miles than many year-old cars did, and it required very little maintenance. Aside from Girard's occasional gig at the college, he and Miriam hardly left the house at all. The pharmacy was within walking distance, and all their doctors were within a few miles of the house. They would go to the supermarket twice a month, but it was still going on six weeks since Girard had filled up the gas tank.

Miriam had not driven since Stacey was a toddler—Stacey was their daughter, their only child—and that was a quarter-century ago. Psychologically, she could not handle the stresses of the open road—all the uncertainty and unpredictability—nor did Girard feel comfortable with her trying. Physically, she was not permitted to. They had not always lived that way, but life was volatile, precious in so many ways. They learned that through the years, and they tried to be self-aware. Minimizing risk was a significant part of that. They were careful to slow down and enjoy the time they had, to not take it for granted. In the blink of an eye, everything could change, and they knew that just as well as anybody.

In their daily lives, tastes were savored. Scents were appreciated. Sights were relished. Sensations were not only felt but experienced through the mind and body. And sounds—well, sometimes life could be unfair; that was the luck of the draw. That was why they appreciated what they had and experienced what they both could together. To them, there was no other way. Togetherness was everything. It was all they had.

When Girard opened the door and pushed into the garage, his heart leaped. Not because of what he saw, but rather what he did not. Wet tire tracks left designs on the concrete, and the garage door was propped open a foot or two from the bottom. The emergency cord was flipped up and dangled from the track above, clearly having been yanked. Even more troubling, the Buick was gone.

CHAPTER THREE: Wednesday

Orange was hot emotion. The brightest of shades promoted positivity and encouragement, which were keys when on the path to emotional healing. Without healing, past disappointments and deep emotional scars weighed heavily on the heart and mind. Orange provided the loving determination needed to help recover and to move forward with one's life, past the grief and repentance.

Girard sat in his chair at the head of the table and stayed there until dark. The bananas on the wall had become so realistic they practically unpeeled themselves. Slithering worms invaded the apples. The vortex spun until Girard's vision blurred and vertigo set in. His head spun right along with it.

He waited for hours, through the morning coffee break, past lunch, beyond supper. He did not move from the chair. His bladder swam. His stomach growled. The nerves in his back pinched.

What he saw in the garage puzzled him. The condition of the door lacked logic. The missing Buick was disturbing. It was not that Girard was afraid Miriam could not handle it, because he knew she could. She was a strong-willed woman, and while she had her limitations and lacked the confidence she once radiated with, she could fend for herself. But Girard still worried about her. It was unlike her to be spontaneous. And taking the car was more than spontaneous; it was reckless. Miriam had never been reckless, not even in her younger days. Which is why Girard knew something was wrong.

But what could he do about it? Miriam did not carry a cell phone—neither did he—so he could not call her. He could go on foot and roam the neighborhood looking for her, but what good would that do? The ground he could cover would hardly be worth the effort. It would be premature to call the police. So Girard sat and waited for Miriam to return, although part of him questioned if she ever would. The Miriam he knew would not have even left it the first place, but there had to have been a reason—the alternatives were too chilling to consider.

But she never came home.

When the clock struck eleven and the night approached its darkest, Girard went to bed. Before he did, he checked the garage again, just to be sure. Nothing was different, just that the tire tracks had evaporated. He left the hall light on, plus the one over the garage and on the front stoop. Miriam would have an explanation for her behavior in the morning, and he was certain it would be a logical one. He did not give it a second thought as he scrubbed his teeth and buttoned up his pajama front.

He lay awake for much of the night. Empty thoughts kept him up. He imagined the hands of a clock rotating on its axis, counted the ticks as the longer of the two hands moved along. He thought of Miriam at times, and of his green house, and of the curious condition of the garage. He counted four hundred and twelve sheep before he fell asleep.

Sometime later, Girard was startled awake by a commotion in the driveway. The bed was still cold next to him, the pillow empty. He slid out from under the sheet and pinched open the blinds, only to find a raccoon scrounging through the garbage barrel like a scoundrel. A tap or two on the window typically got the coon to hurry away, but not on this night. The bandit looked up to the window and stared at Girard with its tantalizing illuminating eyes, then turned back to the barrel and used its claws to shred a garbage bag. Girard rapped on the glass once, then twice, then with both hands simultaneously. The coon did not scurry away until Girard fumbled the window open.

The cracked window let a cold breeze swirl around the bedroom and created a funnel of chill that brushed over Girard's exposed skin and made him shiver. He shut the window and turned his back to it and tried to tempt sleep with darkness. His mind raced. Sheep filled the room, even though he lost count after the third dozen. Morning felt like it would never come.

Girard must have eventually fallen asleep because the doorbell woke him. Confusion was prevalent. He leaned over to shake Miriam awake, only to be reminded of the previous day's events. His fingers wrapped around her pillowcase and pulled it toward his face. The scent was familiar, comforting, almost as if it were really her. Girard imagined it was.

The doorbell rang again, followed by a knock. It was one of those heavy knocks, one of those that came from the side of someone's fist as opposed to the knuckles, one of those that belonged to someone who was not going to leave until the door was answered. Girard tried to yell out that he was coming, but his throat was scratchy, his voice slightly hoarse. His bladder pressed him for relief, but it would have to wait.

The maple creaked beneath Girard's feet as he descended the stairs. The railing was coarse against his hand, the mound in the center raised a splinter above the outer edges, the uneven surface scratchy. Their wedding photograph hung near the base of the stairs, and Girard stopped to admire it. The photo was so faded it was more grayscale than vibrant with rich colors, but the image was still fresh in his mind—the entire day was. It was like a film reel that continuously played, and it just happened to be Girard's favorite scene.

He and Miriam married young but without regret. With their immediate family as witnesses, they recited their vows in a quaint barn a few miles from the town's center. The Justice of the Peace was a mutual friend who offered his services in exchange for a pint of moonshine. The flowers were picked from the fields around town and cost nothing. It was store-bought cupcakes for the guests for dessert. The disc jockey was a run-down transistor radio with a busted antenna.

Girard and his beautiful bride danced until their arches ached, until their faces hurt from all the smiles and jokes and laughs. They stuffed cupcakes in their mouths and poured cheap Champagne down their throats, and they danced until the batteries in the transistor died.

For the first time that night, they made love under the stars. The sun had long since set, the crowd departed. It had not been the first time for either of them, but it was their first time together. The ecstasy was far more than physical—the emotional connection had been on a whole new level that Girard had not known even existed in life. As a tribute to the memories they would never forget, they left Miriam's sundress hanging on a cast iron hook near the rear sliding door and Girard's rented wingtips on the floor beneath. Then they split town in Girard's 1974 Eldorado convertible and never looked back. Girard never did pay the rental fee for the shoes, which always bothered him.

They had met on the street six months prior. Their eyes locked from a distance. As the gap closed between them while they walked from opposite directions, Girard knew right then. Miriam was the most beautiful woman he had ever laid eyes on, and he knew he would wed her. He crossed in front of her, stopped, gave her the biggest, most effortless, genuine smile he could manage. He gave her his name, asked for hers, and said her beauty was unmatched by anyone he had ever seen. Miriam's cheeks turned rosy then, and she thanked him and offered him her hand. Girard insisted he take her out for coffee, and she agreed. They were overwhelmed by love not long after, and the rest was history. Girard never understood where the courage to approach her like that came from.

Their wedding day remained the single greatest highlight of Girard's life. The two genuinely happy smiling faces that looked back at him had him reminiscing. One day many years later, Girard was back in that sleepy town on an unrelated visit, and he detoured out toward the old barn. The beaten path was overgrown and the grass was as tall as the windows would have been, and he remembered the area as if he had been raised there. How could he not? He remembered how freely the stars littered the night, how clear and unrestricted the moon had been, how still everything was. He had imagined it in his dreams on more than one occasion through the years.

When he pulled up to where the old barn should have been, it was no longer there, replaced by ash. To say it was a devastating moment in his life would be an exaggeration, but Girard took it hard. The memory of that day would always be there, but standing in the spot where he and Miriam had pronounced their eternal love for one another and having it no longer be there was not something he was prepared for. It was a sign of how much things had changed, about how different life had become. The once carefree twentysomethings had wound up just as their elders had—old and damaged and longing to reclaim the years of their youth. It was at that moment Girard remembered who he once was, what his dreams for his life were.

Life did not go as scripted.

Memories were a funny thing. The same faded photograph had the power to elicit a wide range of powerful reactions that neither made sense nor did not. Girard recalled those better times regularly when he walked past the photograph, only to be reminded of the desolation he felt when he learned the barn no longer existed. His outward emotions were in check, but inside, his heart ached about it. About everything. It seemed as if he longed for the way things used to be a little more with each passing day.

The doorbell rang again. Girard shook himself. He blinked a few times to clear his vision, though nothing blocked it. His eyes stung with heat. He remembered what it was like to have normal reactions, to be able to laugh or cry or experience real joy or pain. Numbness filled his days.

Girard did not bother peeking outside before he opened the door. Muffled voices spoke behind it, but Girard hardly noticed. He flipped the deadbolt, twisted the handle, and pulled on the door, filling the foyer with the morning. Two men stood on the landing, their black police uniforms crisp, all the wrinkles ironed away. The man on the left had his hat in his hands and kept his attention elsewhere. The one on the right had the rim of his pulled down over his eyes so Girard could hardly see them at all. Behind them both, their cruiser sat idly in the drive, which looked out of place.

Girard looked past the officers, sensed that the neighbors across the way watched from their front porch. Though it was not much of a neighborhood feel—everyone kept to themselves. Girard knew the neighbor's name was Bernard and his wife was Jane, and that they had a grown son, but that was the extent of his knowledge. Neighbors sandwiched either side of the house too, but the aspens did an outstanding job of keeping them isolated. Girard wondered if the police presence might change that today.

The officer with the hat in his hands cleared his throat and said, "Excuse me, sir." His throat was still noticeably dry.

Girard detected how uncomfortable the officer was—his forehead shone with perspiration, his tongue massaged the roof of his mouth as if it were stuck there, and his neck arched downward so he could avoid eye contact—and that made Girard uneasy.

"Is this the Remington household?"

Girard nodded.

"Mr. and Mrs. Girard Remington?"

"Yes."

"Are you Girard?"

"Yes." Girard looked between the two incredibly uncomfortable officers. They were both middle-aged and white, and Girard was surprised they were so nervous.

"Mr. Remington," hatless said. "May we come in?"

Girard shifted uncomfortably. His feet were suddenly frozen, and he realized he had not put on shoes. "What's this about?"

"Sir," the other officer said, using his longest finger to flick his hat up above his eyes, "we hate to tell you this, but there's been an accident."

CHAPTER FOUR

Girard led them to the living room, offered them the sofa. Neither man would look directly into his eyes, as if he were a monster. Girard sensed it, felt it, but was not surprised by it. The officers were not the first people who treated him that way, and he did not blame them. It hardly bothered him anymore—it was nothing like it used to be. The numbness helped him to not care about things that were out of his control, which was an advantage. Maybe the only one.

Girard craved a cup of coffee. Not just any cup, though, but the way Miriam made it. He tried others while out—at the college, the gas station, and once he made his own by dispensing the beans from the plastic casing in the supermarket—but none of those were comparable. Miriam had a special way of making it, some secret ingredient that could not be matched by the blandness of the college café or the cheap brew at the Sunoco or even the fresher stuff from the market—it was the love she added, and that was something only she knew the recipe for. Girard missed his wife.

The two uniformed men sat across from Girard with their hats on their laps and their eyes averted. The younger of the two—he was the one who had first spoken on the stoop—scanned the photographs on the wall and studied them. The older one pretended to fetch for something inside his breast pocket, and Girard got the impression they were stalling.

"Mr. Remington," the older officer began.

"Girard. Just Girard."

The officer nodded and looked down at the small notepad he retrieved from his jacket. "Fair enough. Girard it is."

The officer looked up now, and finally into Girard's eyes. He inhaled sharply as if he had to psychologically prepare himself to look at Girard. Girard knew why—it was hard not to notice.

"Girard, please allow us a moment to introduce ourselves," the older officer said. "My name is Sergeant Bell. This here is Officer Chatham. We work for the Helena Police Department."

Girard looked between the two men, wondered why they continued to stall. He shifted in the chair. It was a relic armchair from his grandmother that did not exactly fit in with the rest of the décor, but Miriam let him have it. It was a faded cream color with tears in the fabric and a large stain on the seat, but Girard refused to have it reupholstered. Preserving its original integrity was important to him, regardless of its condition. It was the one piece of furniture that meant something to him, and he was the only person ever allowed to enjoy it.

"Do you mind if we ask you a few questions?" Sergeant Bell said.

"You said there was an accident?" Girard said.

"We'll get to that. Where were you last night?"

Girard folded his hands. "I was here."

"All night?"

"And all day."

"Where was your wife?"

Miriam.

"Miriam was here in the morning."

"What about in the evening?"

Girard thought about the sequence of events from the previous day, about the unusual garage door situation and the missing Buick, and about Miriam's uncharacteristic behavior. He told Sergeant Bell about it.

When he finished, Sergeant Bell and Officer Chatham glanced at each other with concern, or dissatisfaction, or doubt. The look rubbed Girard the wrong way, made him feel as if there was a secret agenda going on and he was the only person to be in the dark about it. He wondered if the accident they referred to was just a way to get themselves in the door and if there really was not an accident at all.

"Why are you here?" Girard asked. He unfolded his hands and rested his forearms on the arms of his grandmother's chair, drummed his fingertips on the wood. His bare feet were not as chilly as they were before, but his tongue still craved Miriam's brew.

"Why didn't you call us?" Sergeant Bell asked once he broke his eye contact with his partner. His notepad had tens of lines of notes written on it.

"I was going to."

"When?"

"This morning, if Miriam wasn't here when I got up."

"Why didn't you?"

"Because you were already here."

Sergeant Bell wrote another note on his pad. "Does your wife stay out overnight often?"

"Never."

"And you didn't find that unusual?"

"I found it incredibly unusual."

"But you still didn't call us?"

"As I said, I was going to in the morning."

Sergeant Bell only nodded. "Did you try to reach out to her?"

"Miriam. Her name is Miriam."

"Miriam," Sergeant Bell said. "Did you try to reach out to Miriam?"

"She doesn't carry a mobile phone, so no. There was no way to contact her."

"That's unusual, in this day and age."

"Not really."

"Most people carry a cell phone."

"Not everyone."

Sergeant Bell clicked his pen. "I guess not."

Girard crossed his arms over his chest and sighed. The morning was getting late, and his green house needed tending to. He did not much care for the break in his routine. "Why are you here, Sergeant?"

Officer Chatham, who had been silent since the initial interaction on the stoop, finally cleared his throat and leaned forward. "Girard," he said, "we found an abandoned vehicle on the side of Highway 15 early this morning. Are you missing a vehicle?"

"My Buick. Miriam took it when she went out yesterday."

"Did you and your wife have an argument or a disagreement yesterday?" Officer Chatham asked.

"No."

"Is there anyone who can vouch for you, who can confirm your whereabouts yesterday?"

Girard was confused, unsure where the officer was attempting to lead the conversation. "You mean like an alibi?"

"Exactly like an alibi."

"Miriam and I are private individuals. We keep to ourselves."

"So that's a no?"

Girard held back, looked between the two men again. Sergeant Bell had his notepad propped up on his knee and his pen ready. He looked intently at Girard as if he were about to share a classified trade secret. Officer Chatham was surprisingly cool, his face solid and unmoving. He blinked every so often but remained patient.

"Do I need an alibi?" Girard asked. The drumming on the wood was down to a single finger now. He was aware it might make him look nervous, but he could not help it; he was nervous. He began to worry something bad happened to Miriam.

"Can we be honest with each other?" Officer Chatham asked, leaning forward further. He looked too comfortable on the sofa, as if he were in his own living room. Girard did not like that.

"I already am," Girard said. "It would be nice if you two started doing the same."

Officer Chatham shot a glance to Sergeant Bell, who spoke: "A gold 2000 Buick Century was found down an embankment on the side of Highway 15, burned to a crisp. Inside the vehicle was the deceased body of an unrecognizable person. It couldn't even be determined if the body was a man or a woman at first, until a further detailed examination took place."

Girard's heart sped up. He felt a tremor in his hand, a churning sensation in his gut.

"And we'd like to know what you might know about it."

Girard searched for words, but they stuck. Thoughts scattered through his mind in a whirlwind, his vision suddenly blurred. "I . . ." he tried, his emotions absent. "I know nothing."

There was a long silence while the two uniforms glanced at each other and back at Girard, as if they were searching for an untruth. Girard was stiff as stone, numb, unable to feel. Just because it was his Buick did not mean the deceased body was Miriam's. Right? There were dozens of other scenarios in play, though Girard did not have the clarity to consider what they were.

"Would you mind getting dressed and coming with us, Mr. Remington?" Sergeant Bell asked.

Girard nodded because he did not know what else to do. "Where are we going?"

"The morgue."

CHAPTER FIVE

Like a criminal, Girard rode in the back seat of the squad car. He did not much care if the neighbors saw. The car smelled of clean linens, like those that only a Febreze air freshener could offer, and cold dark roast. The coffee in the cabin made Girard crave one even more, and his stomach growled. He had not eaten in more than twenty-four hours now, and he was beginning to feel shaky. The gardens in the green house were on his mind as he looked through his own disheveled reflection in the window. He had not seen himself in months. Seeing himself now, he remembered why he kept the mirrors covered.

The officers stayed mostly silent. Officer Chatham drove while Sergeant Bell studied his notes from the passenger seat. The radio buzzed once or twice with an alert from dispatch. Girard found the dynamic to be strange—the younger officer driving while the older one rode along—but he did not put much thought into it. Seniority must not have meant much in the police world, which Girard knew hardly anything about.

Before they had left the house, Girard threw on some brown corduroys, a light short-sleeved button-up, and his favorite pair of leather loafers. Miriam had gotten them for him as a gift for his birthday last year, and he wore them as often as possible. Miriam gave the best gifts.

Girard smelled the morning on his own breath, tasted it as he swallowed. The stubble on his cheeks and neck was scratchy. There were so many things he had to do this morning, and this entire ordeal threw him for an unexpected loop. But he worried about Miriam's safety above all else.

He could not fathom the idea that Miriam was dead. The police officers said it themselves—they were unable to identify the body—so it could have been anyone. His gut told him it was not Miriam they were headed to see, but he had been wrong before—his gut had also told him he was sober enough to drive that night way back when too, but look where that got him.

Girard tried to imagine what it would be like to live without Miriam, to be alone and lonely and completely isolated from the rest of the world, but he could not. He was unable to imagine tasting the flavors or experiencing the sensations or seeing the sights without her. They had been practically attached at the hip for more than forty years, since they were youngsters. As an adult, Girard did not know what it was like to be alone. As a man, he could not remember what that felt like. And it did not seem realistic to him, even now, despite where he was being driven. There was no way Miriam was gone. It was not her time.

The morgue came into view as the police car drove around the bend. It sat between two high risers in the business district of downtown, in the basement of what used to be an old funeral home. The coroner's office was upstairs, along with the administration offices and filing room and a spare desk for the visiting county pathologist. Girard had never been inside the main building, but he had heard of the details, pieced together by the articles in the newspaper over the years about the place.

He felt a twinge in his chest as the car rolled to a stop and Sergeant Bell and Officer Chatham slipped out. Girard pressed a hand to his chest and held his breath until it passed, then he unbuckled himself and waited for Sergeant Bell to open his door from the outside. Girard slid out and squinted into the morning, then the three of them walked toward the front doors together.

Although the reception area was separated from the section of the morgue that held the bodies, pungent chemicals filled the air. Exposed brick lined the wall behind the woman at the desk, and she seemed unfazed by the odor. Girard's right eye watered just a bit, and the lady behind the desk offered him a look of sympathy. Her lower lip curled just slightly, and her eyes sunk, and she blinked rapidly as if to fight off tears. Girard felt the pressure build up in his chest as the formaldehyde penetrated his lungs.

The teary-eyed brunette made a phone call when Sergeant Bell explained who they were and why they were there, and nobody said a word while they waited. Girard kept his eyes on the room—the exposed brick and the cherry end table and the stack of magazines that showed athletes at the peak of their careers posing in slacks and a blazer—anywhere but another set of eyes. He felt as if he were being watched.

On the far side of the reception area, the only other door popped open and a pretty blonde woman with legs that stretched on for miles stepped toward them. She held out her hand and shook those of the two uniformed men but avoided Girard. She introduced herself without a prefix, which took Girard by surprise—the long white overcoat had him fooled. He did not catch her name.

The doctor lookalike led the way. The corridor was narrow and very white—the walls were only a tint darker than the ceiling, and the tile was the same. Uninspiring fluorescent light fixtures hung from the ceiling and spewed bright white light into the corridor. It felt like a prison, or a mental institution. Girard counted the tiles under his feet as he trailed behind the group.

The door at the end of the corridor seemed like a mile away. Soft chatter surrounded Girard, but none of it was audible. All he heard was high heels clanking against the tile, followed by heavy-heeled boots, and his own voice inside his head as he counted. He counted by twos, leaving the odd numbers untouched, and tried to keep up. By the time he reached forty-four, the boots and the heels stopped. Girard looked up and was no more than a full step away from the door, which disturbed him. He had gotten so lost in his own mind that the time passed him by in a flash, never again to be returned. It was wildly careless of him.

Sergeant Bell asked him if he was ready to enter, which Girard nodded to in response. For a moment, he forgot where he was. Then the door creaked open and he saw the table—it was made of steel and was on wheels—and he remembered. He thought of Miriam and of the accident, and he still could not imagine her being gone. He took step number forty-five and felt immediately out of his element. The odd number made him uncomfortable.

The chemicals hit him hard. It was like opening an oven door once it was warmed to four hundred degrees and being temporarily suffocated by the scalding heat. Girard imagined it was like having his head held underwater for thirty seconds and being unable to breathe, being unable to return to the surface, like a waterboarding interrogation. The smell smothered him where he stood, and he rested his hand against the wall to keep himself upright. Both officers buried their noses into the pits of their elbows. The non-doctor appeared to be unfazed by it, nose blind.

Girard took a minute to gather himself, to regain his composure. His mind was jumbled. He thought he was better off at home, where he could wait for Miriam to arrive, and so he could play caretaker to the green house. The morning feed had long since passed by now.

He looked around. The walls were lined with what looked like shelves of steel caskets, and he thought he felt a chill coming from the far wall. A portable metal table covered with thin paper sat in the center of the room, resting idly, adjacent to the larger one. The smaller of the tables had surgical tools on it—a scalpel, a pair of forceps, scissors, and a strange-looking saw—but they looked unused. Girard could not imagine any of those tools being used on Miriam—or on anyone else, for that. It seemed cruel and inhumane.

Sergeant Bell and Officer Chatham and the unnamed woman—by now, Girard figured she was the coroner—surrounded the larger table. All six eyes were on him while someone spoke. Girard missed it. The black body bag begged for and stole his attention. A mound was underneath it—a mound of a charred corpse, if what the police officers had said was true—and it seemed small. But then again, Girard did not know what a body looked like inside of a body bag, or what a fire might have done to it. He prayed it was not Miriam.

The coroner unzipped the bag. Her fingertips held on to the edge of the aluminum with great precision, or cautiousness. It was as if the zipper contained a deadly infectious bacterium, and merely touching it could transmit the infection to her and invade her body like the plague. The coroner used her off-hand to keep the body bag steady, which was a move Girard found distasteful. Though he could not pinpoint why it bothered him.

Crimson hair peeked through the slit in the bag—the hair was not naturally that color, but disturbingly dyed that way from the accident; the roots were different. Girard's stomach churned.

"Are you alright?" the coroner asked, a strange, satisfying grin on her face. It was as if she were hardened to the blood and gore of death and thoroughly enjoyed seeing someone else being exposed to it that usually was not. Girard thought the woman looked pleasant enough, kind even, but that all changed. Quickly, he disliked her.

He nodded.

The coroner slid her hand further down the bag, toward the blackened feet of whoever was trapped inside, exposing the severed clothing and unrecognizable skin tone. Girard lifted a fist to his lips and pressed it there. He studied the body for a long minute, searched beyond the surface for something that might remind him of Miriam, for some physical attribute that might stand out. He stepped toward the torso and looked hard, tried to find the scar that ran along the underside of Miriam's belly from when she had a cesarean. He studied the corpse's calves and feet and ankles where exposed and tried to locate the birthmark on Miriam's foot. But he found nothing.

"Well, Mr. Remington," Sergeant Bell said. "Do you see anything that might indicate this is your wife?"

"Miriam," Girard said.

"Yes, I know."

The four of them stood in silence for a while. Girard had to avert his eyes before long though, as the corpse in front of him did strange things to his mind he did not much care for.

"No, nothing," he said. "I can't tell."

"What about the clothing?" the sergeant asked. "Do you recognize any part of the outfit?"

Girard shook his head. "No."

"What about tattoos? Scars? Birthmarks?"

"Miriam doesn't have any tattoos."

"Scars? Birthmarks? A missing toe? Anything unusual?"

Girard looked up and made eye contact with the sergeant. He did not appreciate his tone. This was not a game to him. "No," he said. "I can't tell."

Sergeant Bell looked to the coroner and nodded, and she zipped up the bag. Girard felt instantly more comfortable, but still far from it. He needed to get back to the green house.

"Is this your wife, Mr. Remington?" Sergeant Bell said.

"I don't know."

The sergeant nodded again, and this time the coroner left the room momentarily, only to return with a Petri dish with something gold resting inside. She placed the dish on the small table and moved away. Girard felt Sergeant Bell's eyes on him.

"What's this?" Girard asked.

"Do you recognize this?" Sergeant Bell said.

Girard swallowed hard. His vision blurred, as if tears were puddling. But he knew they were not. His chest tightened though, and his airways stuck, and both sensations were real. "Why do you have this?"

"We found it at the scene of the accident," the sergeant said.

Girard reached for the Petri dish and for the gold object inside, his hand trembling. Officer Chatham pulled the dish away before he could grab it.

"Evidence. Sorry," Officer Chatham said.

"Well?" Sergeant Bell tried. "Do you recognize this?"

Girard did not say anything and looked up to the uniforms. The corner still had a sheepish smile that made her look wicked; Sergeant Bell's lips were puckered, his eyebrows narrow, as if he had something to prove; and Officer Chatham seemed hesitant, tucked away further than the other two, looking as if he was unsure about his partner's tactics despite being the one with his hand on the Petri dish.

Girard did recognize the golden object. It was more than just an object—it was a symbol of commitment, of honor, of love. It represented the single greatest day of his life, the summit of his happiness. He reached for his own and spun it, felt the cold metal against the soft part of the underside of his finger. Inside the Petri dish was Miriam's wedding ring, and that meant she was not wearing it. And considering the circumstances, that also meant she was dead.

CHAPTER SIX

Things were different after Girard saw Miriam's wedding ring. It was difficult to deny she was dead, tough to challenge the theory it was her charred body in that body bag. No other theory made sense. Miriam was gone.

Girard had to sit down.

The coroner slid a chair under Girard, and he fell into it. It was made of rigid plastic with a thin cushion on the seat, but Girard hardly noticed. His everything was numb—his emotions, his physical sensations, his intelligence—and he was speechless. Not speechless as in the cliché, though, but physically speechless. He opened his mouth and used his tongue to develop words the same way he had done billions of times in his life, but nothing worked. His tongue felt like a rolled-up carpet in his mouth, and his lips stuck. He formed words in his brain, thought out the ones he wanted to share with the room, but something was off. He felt like a machine in need of greasing, or an engine in need of a tune-up, and he sputtered. His vision clouded.

"Are you alright, sir?" It was the lady coroner. Bangs detached from the pencil bun on her head and swung over her face as she leaned down. The smirk from before was gone now, and her cheeks were flushed.

Girard saw the hazel in her eyes and wondered how he missed them before. They shone like beautiful emeralds in her skull, and Girard saw himself in their reflection. He saw the horror that was his lip, and the skin that had been burned. He remembered the accident from all those years before, relived the anguish, and he thought of Miriam. He closed his eyes and imagined her pain, tried to put himself in her place, tried to imagine what it must have been like a second time.

Inside, he wept at the thought of the agony his dear wife must have experienced, although nobody could have known. He was physically incapable of shedding tears—thanks in part to his ruptured tear duct, but less so than the tranquilizer he was prescribed—and it was more of a handicap than he ever imagined. But it was nothing compared to what Miriam had to live with, and so he rarely felt sorry for himself. And even in those moments when he would loathe in his self-pity and wonder why him, there would be no one there to listen to him, and so that always brought him back to his reality. He did not feel he had the right to complain.

When he opened his eyes again, both uniforms and the pretty blonde were huddled around him. Sergeant Bell snapped his fingers in Girard's face and the coroner fanned him. Officer Chatham held his phone in his hand and fidgeted, as if searching for a contact in his directory.

"Did you find anything else?" Girard managed, his annunciation surprisingly crisp.

"Are you alright?" the coroner said again. She exhaled and her chest sank. Relief swept across her face. "You've been unresponsive."

"Did you find anything else in the car?" Girard tried again as he locked eyes with the sergeant. In the background, the backlight on Officer Chatham's phone dimmed and he pocketed it.

"Like what?"

"Anything."

Sergeant Bell straightened and turned to look at his partner. His shoulders rose, then fell, and he turned back to Girard and said, "No. The vehicle is still in the process of being exhumed. It had fallen down a rather large embankment."

"But, the ring?"

"It was on her person."

"May I see it?"

"See what?"

"The car. The exhumation."

Sergeant Bell turned to his partner again. They quietly chatted among themselves, whispered close enough so only they could hear. Girard waited and said nothing, blinked only when necessary, which was more often than ever these days.

"Mr. Remington," Sergeant Bell began, turning back to Girard, "what you're asking for is an unorthodox request."

Girard stayed silent, waited for more, wanted more. Expected more. But more never came. So Girard stood up. And to the obvious chagrin of Sergeant Bell, Girard brushed past him and started for the door, as if he were the one in charge. Girard stopped when he got to the doorway, then he turned and said, "Are we going, or not?"

#

The experience was indescribable. This portion of Highway 15 was winding. A yellow street sign sat idly, telling drivers the next ten miles would be much of the same. The speed limit dropped by a quarter. The pavement was worn and faded and cracked, and the blacktop had more of a gray hue than black, having been kissed by the sun day after day. Steep cliffs and twisty turns and blind cutoffs ruled this part, and it was no wonder more fatalities did not occur. Stubby bollards connected with thin steel hugged the shoulder, keeping the massive stones that would infrequently break off from the towering cliffs away from the road. If it was supposed to keep drivers protected, it did not. It was obvious which sections were redone to fix the damage of a colliding vehicle. It all made Girard feel sick to his stomach.

This portion of Highway 15 did not have a nickname, though it could have. It was not known as Death Alley or Slaughter Alley or the Road of Death. It was simply Highway 15, but everyone knew how dangerous it was. A nickname was not needed to tell them. No one wanted to acknowledge it, but everyone knew it. Girard certainly did. Now twice over.

One lane was still blocked off, which diverted slow-moving traffic through one lane on the left. A handful of state troopers stood by the rail and admired the wreckage below. Another held a portable stop sign and directed the influx of traffic. The damage was not immediately visible upon initial arrival, but when Officer Chatham's squad car squeezed through the crowd and crept toward the commotion, Girard finally saw it.

Two Bert's Towing trucks were positioned by the breakage in the fencing, their back ends faced the edge of the cliff. Four men in grubby ball caps and greasy jumpsuits stood in a half-circle away from the damage. Each of them took a turn making animated diagrams with their arms as the squad car approached, and it was clear a disagreement was being had. The accident happened hours ago, sometime yesterday, and yet there did not seem to be much progress in extracting the Buick from the ravine. Girard wondered how Miriam's body was recovered so quickly.

Officer Chatham pulled to the side and stopped the car. Both he and Sergeant Bell opened their doors and got out, and one of them opened the back. Girard did not move his eyes from what was left of the section of fence. What used to be waist-high and bolted to the earth was now gone, flattened and split down the center. It looked like fallen chicken wire and did not seem to perform much better. Dark rubber streaks were noticeably absent from the pavement. No shards of broken glass or chunks of metal from the frame were visible. The heavy police presence told him the investigation was far from over. It did not look like it had even begun.

Girard followed the two officers toward the break in the fence. Sergeant Bell rested a hand on Girard's shoulder as they approached, as if they were friends. Girard looked at him for a moment to size up his motivations, then he was introduced to the truck drivers as the victim's husband. He quickly shook all four grimy hands. Girard looked away as the four men continued to chat among themselves. A news van waited on the other side of the barricade of police cruisers, the reporter outside trying her best to absorb enough information to share on the live broadcast later in primetime. Girard got the feeling it would be a long day.

"That's bullshit," one of the tow truck drivers said as he spat at his feet and shook his head.

"I don't hear you making any suggestions," another said.

"Maybe I would, if you shut up and listened for a second."

They all stood quietly for a moment.

"What's the problem here, gentleman?" Sergeant Bell asked. Both of his hands were kept to himself now, old friends no more.

"The vehicle slipped further down the embankment when we tried to pull it out," the tallest one said. His beard was grayer than the others', the skin on his hands more wrinkled. His eyebrows were the bushiest of them all, and the grease stain on his ball cap was the most faded. He was the alpha male of the group, and the other three men stood a smidge shorter than they had before.

Girard shoved his hands in his pockets and stood there, restless. The man in charge filibustered about what happened to the Buick—about how the victim's body was pulled out through the rear window, about how hooking the truck to the frame of the Buick had been deemed to be close to impossible, about how he did not think they had the equipment to yank it from the ravine—but the details were lost. Girard ignored the men and stepped closer to the edge.

The surface below was like a canyon—large chunks of boulders were strewn throughout the side of the hillside, variations of color non-existent; the sandy soil coughed up piles of dust with even the slightest wind gust or sharp claws landing on it. The sun reflected off something aluminum in the ravine and temporarily blinded Girard. He made a visor with his hand but still could not see the bottom, so he turned away. The smell of gasoline singed his nostrils and burned the back of his throat.

A hand landed on his shoulder. Girard turned, and there was Sergeant Bell again, with his head cocked to the side and his lips pursed upward, and he gave Girard a sympathetic glance. Two hours ago, Sergeant Bell was different. He had been confrontational and skeptical and borderline brash. But ever since the events in the morgue, things had changed. Girard felt it then—he could tell the difference in his mind, felt the pain in his heart— and now he felt it again. This time it came from the sergeant directly, and his eyes looked pained too.

For the first time, Girard felt like a victim. He felt like a widower, like a lonely soul bound to spend his days in silence and solitude. He thought of Miriam and her smile, and of her inward beauty and her outward exquisiteness. He thought about how much he missed her already. And when he looked into the sergeant's eyes and recognized the sympathy within them, Girard knew his life would never be the same again.

CHAPTER SEVEN

It took hours for the Buick to be exhumed. The morning turned into afternoon, and the afternoon turned into evening. Temperatures rose, then fell. The crowd on the other side of the barricade shrunk around lunchtime, then grew and multiplied later in the day. Girard stood and watched the whole event. He let his mind wander.

The first time he experienced something like this was thirty-seven years ago. He never thought it would happen again, did not think it was possible. He had just turned thirty then. Miriam was three years older. They had been married for eight happy years. Stacey was seven.

Times were different in the 80s. Safety was not as of a priority as it was today. Not a day went by when Girard did not wonder how his life would have even different if there was a side airbag equipped. He drove a compact car at the time, and one of the reasons it was less expensive than its counterparts was the safety features. Balding tires, slick roads, and limited visibility were the leading factors that night. Not to mention the other influences that were in play too—those were kept quiet, locked away, to be brought to the grave.

As far as Girard was aware, there were only a handful of people on the planet who knew what happened that night. Miriam struggled with recollecting the full details at times, but not Girard—he knew exactly what happened, remembered the full vivid imagery as if it happened yesterday. The memories still haunted his dreams at night, still woke him in a panic, drenched with sweat, thick with guilt. The tranquilizer kept the dreams at bay sometimes, but the alternative side effects took a toll on his body. More than his body, even, was the effect the drug had on his mind. He could think all the thoughts he always had, could remember the bad days and the good ones and the nightmarish ones. He could still remember the sights and smells and tastes and sounds of that night, and he hated that about himself.

As he stood near the edge of the cliff and watched the trucks hook on to the Buick at the bottom of the ravine for the umpteenth time without success, he wondered how he would fare. His mind was already fragile and unforgiving of himself, and he knew he had to find a way to convince himself this was all his fault. If only he had been a better communicator with Miriam and would have known what was on her mind, would have known what drove her to get behind the wheel yesterday; if only he had gone out looking for her, maybe there could have been a way to stop this from happening; or if only he had been a better man thirty-seven years ago, none of this would have ever happened in the first place. He was hard on himself, relentless. Doctor Brown had her work cut out for her.

Come noon, Sergeant Bell offered to buy Girard lunch, but he declined. Many jumbled thoughts ran through Girard's mind, but hunger was not one of them. While the men from Bert's pulled out their coolers and ate the sandwiches their wives made for them before the sun came up, Girard stood and waited. The hottest part of the day was still to come, but Girard was determined to stay for as long as it took. The Buick would be kept for evidence, he knew, but he wanted to see it firsthand. He needed to. Something about the whole situation still felt off somehow, as if there was just a big misunderstanding or a case of mistaken identity. But if he saw the Buick up close with his own two eyes, he might believe it was true. Then he might accept that the Jane Doe he saw still in the body bag at the morgue was his wife—his precious, darling Miriam.

By late afternoon, there was a breakthrough. Bert's men rigged together a pulley system with their hooks, and though the stretching of the chains tested the welds, slowly but surely, the Buick was brought to the surface. A murmur came from the crowd of bystanders as the now charred mid-size sedan was pulled from the wreckage. The glass was gone from the rear windshield, replaced by a gaping hole that Girard knew his wife's corpse was pulled out from. He shuddered at the thought of her being treated that way, of her body being manhandled like an object rather than a capsule for her beautiful soul. Just because her body was lifeless did not mean she was dead. The soul lived on—at least that was what Miriam believed. Even still, Girard was thankful the rescue team had gotten her body out in time, before the Buick slipped further down the embankment.

It hit him then, as he saw the Buick, that everything was real. What he experienced was really happening, and the woman he saw at the morgue was, in all probability, what remained of his wife's body. Miriam was gone.

Girard's knees buckled, and he fell to the ground. Sergeant Bell was nearby and rushed over to him, as did Officer Chatham and a trio of first responders who had been there for much of the day. Girard was shaded and fanned and offered ice water, but he spent more time swatting away the intruding hands than he did accepting the help. From behind him, someone slid their forearms underneath his armpits and lifted him back to his feet. The crowd of bystanders was noisy now, and Girard saw more than a handful of flashbulbs go off as he made his way toward the ambulance. He did not enjoy all the attention he received, but the words to say so were elusive. He almost felt humiliated by it all.

An hour passed—or maybe it was less than that, Girard was unsure—and one of the trucks that helped exhume the Buick from the ravine pulled away from the scene with it. Sergeant Bell said something to the dispatcher over his radio about it going to the warehouse garage that was the property of the police department, and Girard knew that meant he would probably never see it again. He was not sure what the next step for him would be.

Much of the crowd cleared out after that. Camera operators packed up their gear and piled into news vans. Civilian bystanders put their arms around their loved ones and held them close. The state police and local force shook hands and went in separate directions after a job well done. Girard insisted he would be all right, and so the fire trucks and lone ambulance departed and drove out of sight, leaving a trail of dust in their rearview. When the pandemonium cleared and the sun began to fade behind the roaring hills in the horizon, Girard looked around and took in the scene, tried to process everything. One news van remained along with his ride, and he was glad to not be alone. Even as the long-legged reporter strutted her way toward him with the camera crew in tow, Girard did not mind.

Sergeant Bell met the woman halfway and said something to her and her crew, but they did not back down. Girard yelled out that it was okay, which caused a stir. The reporter and her men rushed toward Girard as if he might change his mind at any moment. Sergeant Bell gave Girard a look that begged the question of his certainty about this, but Girard ignored him. He blindly answered the woman's questions until he was too numb to comprehend what she asked, and that was when the sergeant stepped in and wrapped it up. Girard was thankful for that.

Without another word, Sergeant Bell, Officer Chatham, and Girard all piled into the squad car and left the scene for good. Not a single word was spoken on the ride back, the undeniable truth hovering over them like a black hole. It was a somber day.

The night that followed was unquestionably the single most depressing, lonely night of Girard's life. At least thirty-seven years ago, Girard had Miriam. While maybe not in the way he wanted or needed, she was there. He was able to hold her hand and kiss her knuckles and stroke her hair and smell her skin. But now, as Girard unlocked the front door to the darkened house and pushed inside, everything was so empty. The living house felt huge and overwhelming for just him. Girard's thoughts were futile and hollow. And most of all, his heart was bruised and battered, and without the one person in his life that made it whole. Girard loved his wife more than anything in the world, and he thought the pain of missing her might kill him.

#

For the first hour, he did nothing. He sat at the dining room table, stared at Miriam's empty chair, and silently wept dry tears. The bones crunched around his heart and left him gasping for fresh breath. His larynx pulsated as he strained to hold back the screams of devastation that invaded his soul like a demon. He tried but could not imagine living his life without Miriam next to him, holding his hand, rubbing her thumb along the inside of his wedding ring. For all they had been through in more than forty years together, they had an unspeakable bond. They did not talk about the hardest of times but rather spent their days relishing the best of times. There was only one thing that could ever break the bond they had, and it came much too quickly. Girard thought he still had ten, maybe fifteen or even twenty more years to prepare for the inevitable separation. And frankly, he needed more time with her.

Girard had a way out, an escape from the imminent misery that would inevitably overtake his life and smother him, and he considered it. Hard. He had a dozen pills left, which ought to do it. He thought of Stacey and wondered what she would think about it and about him once it was done. They had not spoken much in the last decade, ever since she found out the truth about what happened thirty-seven years ago, when she was just a child herself—although what she thought she knew was only part of it, with the other half being so much worse. In many ways, Girard did not blame her for not wanting to be part of his life—what he did was unforgivable. Miriam, somehow, had found it in her heart to forgive him. Girard had spent every day since making it up to her the best way he knew how, although it never felt like enough. Miriam was a special type of woman. A rarity.

Girard sat on the bathroom floor with the orange bottle rolling in his palm, the cap unscrewed. The dozen looked more like a hundred and he stared down the cylinder that went on forever. He had a cup of water nearby, resting on the edge of the bathtub. The curtain Miriam had him hang brushed against his arm and reminded him of everything he had lost. And that one simple brush took away his will to keep on living. He would not be strong enough to cope.

He poured the entire bottle into his hand and watched as three or four pills from the top spilled onto the floor beneath him. The pills bounced like soft pillows as they crashed to the tile and tempted him with the darkness. It was the only way to get rid of the pain. And he had so much pain. It finally won.

Stacey would be indifferent—that was what he determined at that moment. The possibility of it being shortsighted was real, but Girard did not care about that. Without Miriam in his life, logic could be discarded. His work meant nothing. He made no real connections with any of his students and chose not to associate with his colleagues. Stacey, his only child, was hardly in his life at all. Miriam was his only friend, his soulmate, his everything, and now she was gone. And so he had nothing to live for.

It was time.

He lifted a hand to his mouth and pressed the first pill to his lips. The casing felt elasticized against him, the smell total nothingness. He willed himself to open his mouth and welcome in the permanent darkness, to drown out his misery, but his lips would not part. He tried and tried until his face ached and his jaw locked with tension, but something inside him would not let him do it. And he did not understand why that was. He wanted it so badly, for the pain to end, but he could not do it, he just could not.

What stopped him?

It was hard to pinpoint, exactly, but it was something real. Maybe it was the voice of the beyond that spoke to him, or perhaps it was something less foreign, something less mystical. As it turned out, it was something more simplistic than that. It was only meant to be a detour, a simple delay of the inevitable. If he chose to end his suffering before his given time, he needed to ensure he was prepared if he met Miriam on the other side. There were affairs that required order first.

Not a single day passed whereas Girard did not pick Miriam a flower from her garden. Tuesday's pink rose was still in the vase downstairs, and a fresh one was long overdue. He could smell it—the freshness of the petals that begged to be picked, the moistness of the soil that fed their labyrinth of roots, the coolness of the perfectly crisp filtered air inside the green house. Wednesdays were for marigolds, and that had been the same for years. He would end it all with the orange marigold in his hand so he could have something to present to Miriam if he crossed over. Or he would go up in flames with the marigold in his clutches, and the flame would burn even hotter. He deserved whatever it was he was destined for, no matter how horrible the possibilities were.

Except that was not what happened. Something remarkable happened instead: The green house saved Girard's life. For the second time.

CHAPTER EIGHT

Girard sat on the stone with his gardening shears in one hand, Miriam's marigold in the other, and wept dry tears until his eyes ached. They were so dry he thought he might tear holes through his eyelids when he blinked. Without needing to look, he could tell his cheeks were swollen as if he had just gone the distance in a prizefight. He never thought he would beg for tears, but that was exactly what he did.

Nose down, Girard jammed the shears into the tile and shrieked. He screamed to the God he once knew, to the God he thought he was supposed to know. He begged for his forgiveness, for him to give Miriam another chance at life, to take Girard instead. The plastic cylinder rolled against his thigh and dug into his flesh as he pounded on the tile, always tempting. The casings rattled inside as Girard shook, tormented him, dared him to indulge, to give in to his most scandalous desires. Girard clenched his eyes shut and screamed until his throat hurt, until he was physically exhausted. And when he had nothing further to give, he gave in and collapsed against the cold.

When he awoke, nothing was different. The shears were still clutched in his right hand, the marigold in his left. The green house was still 76.4 degrees and he was still breathing. And Miriam was still dead. But he felt better, calmer than he was before. It was as if the weight of the world had been lifted off his shoulders, as if the burden of his sins had been pardoned. As if he was able to press onward for a while longer.

Girard stood and looked at his watch. He lost track of time hours ago, but the lack of darkness through the glass ceiling told him it was late in the afternoon and not early in the morning. He pocketed the shears and pressed a finger into the pits of his eyes and blinked. Exhaustion smothered him.

Back inside the living house, Girard sat at the dining room table and caught his breath. It was disturbingly quiet. The hands on his wristwatch ticked. The refrigerator hummed in the next room as the generator inside it kicked on. Girard's stomach grumbled. Something was different—he felt it. What it was he could not say, but it was there. It was unmistakable. He had found an inner strength while in the green house, during his weakest moments. Most amazing of all, the marigold was undamaged during his outburst. The stem was stiff and intact, the sepals curled. The marigold shone like it never had before, the orange never brighter. It was cheery, almost hopeful, as if it tried to tell Girard everything would be all right. And for some reason, he believed it.

It was as if Miriam had reincarnated as the wondrous flower and spoke to Girard, encouraged him, gave him the strength to move on. Girard wondered if it was the universe finally answering him, somehow giving him a sign that he would be okay without her. But Girard did not know if he could believe in that. He did not know that he could not though, either, and that kept him interested. Whatever it was, something remarkable happened inside the green house, and there was no questioning that. Without its lure, he would have been dead already, surrendered to his demons, lying face down on the cold bathroom floor. Its powers were undeniable.

Girard pushed himself to his feet and laid the marigold on the table. He carried the vase to the kitchen and discarded the day-old rose, then cleaned and replaced the water in the vase. The pills in his pocket no longer seemed needed, so he left the bottle in the corner cabinet and turned back for the dining room. The marigold fell into the vase as if it were meant to be there, swayed from side to side before coming to a rest in the center. It was a minuscule detail, but one he took notice of. If it was the voice of the universe that spoke to him, or if Miriam had been reincarnated as the most beautiful plant on earth, Girard believed it could happen. For the first time. Maybe it was nothing, or maybe it was something more, but in life, Miriam was always the center of Girard's. She kept him centered as a person, kept him grounded, kept him humble. And even when she disagreed with the choices he made or experienced frustration over the flaws he had, she was always there for him, directly in the center of his chest, a companion for his heart as the lifeblood of his existence.

Girard almost smiled. He felt at peace. He was ready to continue living, to somehow start to rebuild after the biggest tragedy of his life—and that was significant. Girard went to the kitchen and did something he had not done in more than forty years: He made a meal. And it was not awful.

Making a meal was one thing—a distraction for his mind, if nothing else— as was eating to some extent. When it became difficult again was after he ate, after his plate was cleaned and his stomach was full. The distractions were gone. It was just him now, alone, his only company the silence of the four walls that suffocated him.

The marigold sat beautifully in the center of the table, and Girard stared at it with admiration. His mind wandered. He thought back to the night when everything changed—to when he became who he was now, to when Miriam became who she was. He thought about that night almost daily, always in his dreams, whether he wanted to or not.

It was blustery. Or maybe that was too cliché, maybe even inaccurate to some extent. The sidewalks were packed with snow. Brown and white heaps of it was pushed in piles wherever it fit. The roads were recently plowed, but the temperature had fallen fast. The coldest part of the evening was approaching.

Miriam had hooked her arm onto Girard's as if she had caught him fishing, and she laughed deep belly laughs at his jokes. Everything he said was funny that night; she glowed with the delight of an enjoyable evening and the happiness of life's gifts. Despite the below-freezing chill outside, inside the car was steamy. The dashboard vent was cranked up to high and the rubber wipers squelched back and forth over the frozen glass. It felt like a sauna, smelled like lust.

Miriam tossed her head back and forced out a laugh that struck Girard as genuinely jubilant, and he smiled back. Her naturally aligned teeth were as white as the embankments outside, and her lips were outlined in ruby so deep it would have made Marilyn Monroe look twice. He gave her a once-over as her excitement rose along with the pitch of her laugh. His eyes shifted from what he saw through the murkiness to the exceedingly distracting scarlet that radiated from Miriam's face, then back to the road again. He could not help himself.

Girard left one hand on the wheel and used the other to pull Miriam close to his chest. Her hair slid through his fingers like silk as he dug into her skin and kissed her. Time slowed. The FM dial rang with the raspy grit of Conway Twitty's Midwestern twang, but it was even more drawn out than usual. Chills ran through Girard's body like electricity when the tip of Miriam's tongue grazed over his, and his thighs convulsed when she placed a hand between his legs and stroked him. Miriam whispered in his ear and pulled away, grinned at him, unknowingly licked her lips in a way that drove Girard wild.

But her expression quickly fell off.

Girard turned back to the road and his vision blurred. Everything spun around him. Miriam clutched onto his hand and made a sound that no man should have to hear his wife make. Girard whipped the steering wheel to the left as far as it would go, then back to the right, and the car torpedoed into one of the guardrails that were meant to save lives.

What happened after that changed everything. But Conway Twitty kept on as if nothing was wrong, and Girard never forgave him for that.

The phone rang. Girard spun in his chair in a panic, startled not only by the bell that jingled from the wall but also from the detail of his daydream. His everything trembled, and he was drenched with sweat. The visions of that night were as lifelike as they were in his dreams during sleep, and for a second, he thought he could taste the ecstasy of his wife's lips again. And then he heard that fucking song, and he thought he might be sick.

What a shame, what a sight. A good love died tonight.

Girard let the phone ring.

CHAPTER NINE: Thursday

Red was passion. It was fiery desire, intense love. Love for others is what gave man strength and a reason to live. The deepest of love was an unbreakable bond where, no matter the circumstances, two people would remain joined as one through mind, body, and soul. This love would strengthen as the years passed, never weakening, and always take precedence in their lives. The words of love must not be spoken, as their unitedness may be known by them and only them, and was not necessarily on display for others to admire or envy.

The phone rang three additional times throughout the night. Girard ignored them all. The final call came just minutes after nine o'clock. Girard imagined reporters on the other end, weighed down by the pressures from their editors who needed a quote from the lonely soul on the broadcast. He considered if Miriam's accident might be the top story of the day, but he hoped not. He did not need the entire world to know about his tragedy. He regretted talking to the reporter.

After the phone stopped ringing for the third time, Girard made sure it would be the last time. He tore the phone cord from the wall and left it dangling in a pendulum near the baseboard. The plastic tip clicked each time it swung past, ever so slightly brushing up against the wood. It would be the only sound Girard would hear for the rest of the evening.

He lay awake for most of the night, physically unable to sleep and mentally not willing to. The nightmare he knew he would have was still fresh on his mind from earlier, and he did not think he had the capacity to experience it again today. There was only so much tragedy one man could experience in a single day before he reached his breaking point, and Girard recognized how close he already was.

He thought again about the pills. There was still time for him to change his mind, and it would be painless. But painless seemed unfair, considering all Miriam had been through, and so that did not seem right. That would be the easy way. A cop-out. Girard deserved to suffer like his wife did, deserved to experience the same anguish as she. He would pay for it for all of eternity if he tried to cheat death. What he truly deserved would come to him in time.

As if it were déjà vu, a ringing doorbell awoke him again. Somehow sleep had overcome his psyche, and Girard was startled awake by just the chime, and not a nightmare. He lay motionless for a minute, giving his mind a chance to catch up, to process what was happening. A chill strangled the air this morning, and Girard found himself wrapped up tight with the bulky comforter pulled up to his chin. The tip of his nose was cold, the inside crusty.

A car door closed somewhere nearby. On the other side of the glass, Girard heard the flapping of youthful morning wings. They were full of energy, fluttering at their peak for the day, excited for their next catch, for the day ahead. There was an excitement about the morning that Girard envied. It was an enthusiasm that only the young could have, before they knew how life really was, before they discovered how cruel the world could be.

He remembered being like that—eager and lively and optimistic. Optimism was the key—that was difficult to get back once it was lost. In youth, there was nowhere to go but up, nothing less to strive for than the stars and all the universe's possibilities. But then a person hit a point in their life where they accomplished all they set out to, or all they were realistically capable of. Or worse, a tragic event occurred that completely altered one's perspective of the world and of their own life, and their once idealistic aspirations now seemed frivolous. One's optimism could turn to pessimism in a flash when that happened, and then everything outside that realm of realism seemed superficial. It was a tough lesson, but it was the truth. What was fascinating was how people responded to their new reality once they came to realize it. Those who adhered to this actuality were the ones who still saw enough water in the glass to want to make a positive impact—they were the ones who succeeded. And for everyone else? Life was not so easy sometimes. Girard was one of those.

Girard forced himself out of bed. The floor was cold to the touch. His toes scrunched. He lacked the motivation to even peek out the glass, was without the desire to care. Part of him wondered if it was those two police officers again, back to bring good news this time. Maybe they miraculously found Miriam alive somewhere—what if the woman in the body bag was not her? Maybe it was all one big misunderstanding. Perhaps yesterday was all but a dream, a cruel way for his mind to play tricks on him to torment him even further. The mistakes of his past would never leave his conscience, and so maybe this was one of the ways it would manifest itself—in a torturous, lifelike dream where the imagery was just an illusion. He wondered if it was possible for the medication to mess with his mind like that.

His pace sped up as he approached the stairs. A glimmer of hope sprung into him. What if yesterday was all just a figment of his imagination? He tried to recall the scene in the morgue with vividness, strained his mind to remember what had happened. The Jane Doe was blackened beyond reasonable recognition—Girard recalled that much. The body's rancid odor had overwhelmed him to the point of being distracted, so much so he was unable to spend any real time assessing the body. If he only had more time, undistracted time, to be with the body—to touch its skin and slide his fingers in between its, to press his chest against its—maybe he could make a better judgment. What if it was not Miriam?

Girard nearly stumbled as he leaped off the bottom step. The house felt eerily empty this morning—the paint on the walls dull and bleak, the hung portraits noticeably more depressed than usual—and Girard knew why. He felt it too. This was Miriam's home, her sanctuary, and it was not the same without her. Nothing would be the same without her.

When he reached the front door, Girard's chest thumped. The anticipation of what could be pressed him onward. With his hand on the doorknob, his palm swallowed the brass as if it was insignificant, and Girard froze. He closed his eyes and allowed his lashes to gently touch to the point where his vision was blurred. Light surrounded him, but he could only see darkness. The backsides of his eyelids were perfectly solitary and sent him, for a moment, into seclusion. Fresh breath entered his nasal passages and filled his lungs with a coolness that was seldom not taken for granted. He knew he was fortunate to be alive and that each day was precious, but sometimes his brain forced him to think differently. He struggled with himself daily and had for decades. What got him from one day to the next was Miriam, as she urged him to strive for happiness. But if she were gone, what would that mean for him?

It was she who inspired the green house, and it was her essence that kept it going. Between the daily flowers and the smiles she would offer in return, her spirit is what Girard yearned for. More than that, Miriam was who he needed. It was not the language she used or the words she spoke, because that seldom happened, but it was instead her presence. Miriam had a way about her that was unspeakable—both literally and figuratively—but even just her existence was enough. When Girard was around her, he felt complete, whole, as if he had a reason to keep fighting. He was yet to know what being without her for any significant period of time was like, but if each day going forward was anything like the day before, Girard knew he would not be around for long. Without Miriam, Girard was nothing.

He held his breath, and with it, hoped for a miracle.

He twisted the doorknob.

On the other side of the door was an unexpected sight. The breath crept out from his aging lips, and with it, the remaining sliver of hope he had left. It was not the two police officers behind the door, nor was it Girard's dear Miriam.

Girard scanned the woman from head to toe, surprised at how much of a woman she was. He still remembered her as a girl—a young, opinionated, irrational girl—and it had been years since he had seen her. She had hardly spoken to Girard at all in recent years, but her reasons for doing so were far different than Miriam's. The woman stared at Girard as if he were a monster, a behemoth beast who had intruded on her life as if he were a virus. Red streaks laced her eyes and spoke more than words ever could, and Girard did not know what to say to her, even though he had no choice but to produce something.

CHAPTER TEN

It was Stacey. Girard's daughter.

"What are you doing here?" was what he managed to say.

Not exactly welcoming.

But it was no surprise, Girard was not happy to see her. Stacey had been a stranger since she was old enough to make her own decisions, and she abandoned him and Miriam when they needed her support the most.

"I've been calling you," Stacey said, just as coldly as ever.

"Have you?"

"Last night, multiple times."

Girard shrugged, remembered last night when he pulled the plug. He assumed it was reporters at the time.

"What's going on?" she said.

It was a loaded question. How long had it been? Five, six, maybe seven years since he had seen her last? Lots had been going on.

"Why are you here?" he said. He folded his arms and felt a light gust graze his skin. The morning smelled of sunshine and fresh-cut grass and cherries—there was a bush a yard or two into the brush behind the green house.

Her shoulders fell. "I saw you on the news."

Girard kept his arms folded and looked at her good, like he had not for many years. She looked different—not only physically, but emotionally too. He had a knack for recognizing emotional distress in someone. The signs were subtle if you did not know what you were looking for, but as obvious as black if you were. It was the wrinkles under someone's eyes, and the heavy bags. It was the unmistakable look of being overtired, but not due to the lack of sleep or from being overworked. New mothers had a similar look, but they had an excuse. The emotionally distressed were exhausted from the struggle they had to do battle with within their own heads—that was difficult to understand unless you had experienced it yourself, and those who had not may not ever.

Girard knew the look because he had it too. He chose not to look at mirrors anymore because the reflection that stared back would make him feel somber—he very much disliked the person he saw. But during those rare moments when he did unintentionally catch a glimpse of himself, he was reminded of that look. And that look would never let him forget about his daily struggles, as if he ever could, and he had to think about that night all those years ago. So he avoided mirrors at all costs, covered them up with old sheets or blankets or towels.

Stacey had that look.

Whatever demons had intruded her life in these last years, she struggled badly with them. Girard felt sorry for her, but he was not sympathetic. She had made the choice to isolate herself from the rest of the family, so as far as Girard was concerned, that meant she was on her own with whatever she dealt with. Though he would never wish ill upon her.

"Is it true?" Stacey asked, the red streaks in her eyes illuminated as if she were a wick surrounded by wax. "About mom?"

Girard did not know what to say. He was not convinced that was the case, yet he could not be sure it was not either. What could he possibly say?

"You saw the news," he said as he uncrossed his arms.

Stacey covered her face with her hands and began to sob. Uncontrollably at times.

It was an awkward moment for Girard. While estranged, Stacey was his only offspring, his only remaining flesh and blood. And while it was true he disliked the adult she became, he also felt obligated to have love for her. Whether he felt that way about her or not anymore was difficult to define, but that was the same for many of his emotions. Whether to comfort her tore at him.

"Maybe we should go inside and talk," Girard said. "If you want."

Stacey nodded and stepped forward. Girard slid to the side, pressed his back against the door, and let her pass. He caught a waft of her shampoo, which was so faint it could have been two or three days old, and it reminded him of her younger years. Her look had changed and the brown roots that stuck out of her scalp ran to blonde after an inch, but it was still her. She smelled like she used to, underneath the mask of old fruit, but it had no effect on Girard. He smelled it and thought of her as a girl, before she left, and felt nothing.

He reached for his neck and expected to feel the strain from tense muscles. But they were not. The knot in his chest never came. His heart rate failed to speed up. His wind stayed steady. More than anything in the world, aside from Miriam's miraculous return, Girard wanted to feel again. The ability to hurt was taken for granted by those who could, and rightfully so. Nobody thought they were ever going to lose the ability to experience emotion, so who could blame them? They did not know how lucky they were.

Girard followed Stacey to the living room. He sat in his grandmother's chair, she on the sofa. The scene was eerie in its similarity to the day before—when the police officers knocked on the door and sat on the same sofa, a similar somber look on their faces, and told him what they found; now Stacey. Girard thought about that for a moment, allowed it to settle.

Yesterday was definitely real, was it not?

Stacey wiped tears from her eyes and leaned forward, used her hands for support. Her face was ashen, her tone dull, and she looked ten years older than she truly was. Girard looked hard and thought he saw some grays intertwined with her bogus blonde locks that he had not seen in the light before. She had aged prematurely, and it was difficult to look at, even though she was estranged. She was, after all, his only daughter.

"What happened?" Stacey asked with sad eyes.

What did happen?

Girard tried to remember. He shut his eyes for a moment and ran through yesterday—through the police officers' arrival, the visit to the morgue, the scene on Highway 15. The memory of the Buick being hauled out of the ravine as if it were the trophy catch of a deep-sea excursion rang true. He recalled the day with clarity now. The details were too precise to have been a delusion, the agony he experienced too real.

Then it hit him. He often complained about not being able to feel, and it was true. But at a time like this, a time of intense grief, he apparently could. The pain he felt was genuine. It was a breakthrough in some ways, something he and Doctor Brown had worked toward for years, but Girard instantly regretted ever having wished it upon himself. The anguish he felt was so severe he found himself short of breath.

Girard pressed a hand to his chest and dug his fingers into his flesh as if they were talons, pinching to the point of nearly breaking the skin. His chest filled with a heaviness that he imagined one might feel if drowning. His pectorals clenched to the brink of spasming. It was happening.

Girard could not concentrate, but his eyes met with Stacey's, and he saw her expression change. The sadness turned to curiosity, the curiosity turned to confusion, then fright. She leaped to her feet and approached Girard as if she could help him, but he knew she could not. It was not the first time this had happened, and so he knew what to do.

"Dad, are you alright?" Stacey was frantic.

Girard tried to speak but could not. All his energy was tied up in trying not to lose control of himself. His fingers closed around the fibers of his undershirt as he threw his head back and clenched his eyes shut.

"What's happening?"

His eyes remained closed, but Girard sensed Stacey was starting to panic. Her shoes pattered on the floor as if she were walking in circles, lost like a baby wolf that had separated from the pack.

"Get . . . the . . . phone," Girard managed to squeeze out. His throat burned.

"I'll call 911!"

Girard shook his head, unsure if Stacey saw him.

Stacey moved into the kitchen. There was a thrashing for which Girard imagined Stacey fumbling to plug the phone back into the wall plate. The cord was nearby but he could not remember specifically what he did with it.

"No . . . 911," Girard tried.

"What did you say?" Stacey's voice was suddenly loud and clear, her having reentered the room.

"No . . . 911."

"Who then?"

"Michelle . . . Br . . ."

"Who? Michelle who?"

"Bro . . ."

Girard heard Stacey nervously tapping her fingers against something hard, maybe plastic.

"Bro . . . wn."

"Michelle Brown?" Stacey said. "What's her number?"

Girard removed his hand from his chest and pointed to where he thought the kitchen was. An emergency contact list was magnetized to the side of the refrigerator, and her number was labeled on it. He phoned her frequently. It was only seconds before Girard heard the beeps of the phone being dialed. He knew it would be over soon.

"It's ringing," Stacey said as she reentered the room again.

Girard spread his fingers and held out his hand. His eyes remained closed.

"Doctor Brown speaking," came the faint voice from inside the speaker on the phone.

The rigid plastic of the phone fell into Girard's now sweaty palm. He pulled it toward his lips.

"He . . . lp," he said, his voice so hoarse and sickly it frightened even him.

"Girard, is that you?" came the voice again. "Is it happening again?"

Girard shook his head, knew that was the best he could do. Any words he had left stuck to his tongue, which felt like it was ballooning with each passing moment. A quick wave of nausea came and went.

"Okay, don't worry," Doctor Brown said, as calmly as ever. "I'm here, Girard. Stay with me."

Girard nodded.

Stacey sobbed somewhere over his shoulder.

CHAPTER ELEVEN

It was not the first panic attack Girard had endured, and he was certain it would not be the last. While he knew they were overwhelming to experience, he always imagined they were scary for someone else to witness, perhaps even more so than the experience itself. Now he knew that was true. Miriam saw them so often she had grown accustomed to them. Her reactions had become instinctual. It was clear Stacey had not been through it before. She seemed spooked.

Stacey sat with him in the reception area of Doctor Michelle Brown's office and did not say much. Him either. There somehow was not much to say, even after their ordeal at the house. The attack had subsided, although he felt an impingement under his rib cage where he knew the knot sat, patiently waiting for its chance to strike again when the timing was right. It was an intruder in his life that wreaked havoc on him, and while he knew there was very little he could do on his own to stop it from happening, looking at it that way—as an intruder—seemed to help. Doctor Brown took care of the rest.

She always knew just what to say. As Girard's psychiatrist, Doctor Brown was trained in all the modern psychotherapy methods the psychiatry world used, and that made her unique. She was a bit of a throwback in that she was not only able to prescribe medication to her patients, but she also performed psychotherapy as an alternative method of treatment as well—she was both a medical doctor and a licensed clinical psychologist. She had performed psychoanalysis on Girard years ago and garnered a great deal of information on what made him tick, and it had proven to be beneficial. Whenever Girard would have a panic attack he was unable to gain control of, he would call her on her emergency line and she would know just what to say to calm him down. It worked every time, enough so that the panic attack would subside.

The only prerequisite she had about this—she did not give out the emergency number to all her patients—was that Girard must go straight to her office afterward, so they could talk. The arrangement was the furthest thing from a quandary—Girard very much enjoyed speaking with her, and he usually found a bit a temporary relief after they chatted.

Girard stood up when he caught of glimpse of Doctor Brown as she approached from the corridor. Stacey joined him. Although he did not say it, he would have preferred she not be there with him at all. Her presence made him feel antsy.

There were no pleasantries shared between Girard and Doctor Brown—they were not necessary. Through her leopard print framed glasses, her eyes met with Girard's, and he started toward her. He hoped she did not notice Stacey next to him, or at least not say anything. Doctor Brown was the one person outside of his marriage that knew about the depths of the conflict between Girard and his daughter, and he could not imagine what Doctor Brown might say to her that would not expose that.

Girard kept his neck craned and averted his eyes as he followed Doctor Brown past the reception desk and into the carpeted corridor. He sensed Stacey at his heels but did not stop or turn back to confirm. When Doctor Brown's office came into view—the door propped open just enough for someone to pass through, the windows covered with room darkening blinds, a compact white noise machine howling from the top of a knee-high end table near the door—Girard stopped and waited for an invitation to enter.

But instead of inviting him in, Doctor Brown turned to Stacey and said, "I'm sorry, but this is as far as you can come."

"I'd like to join," Stacey said.

"I'm sorry," Doctor Brown tried again, "but you are?"

"I'm his daughter, Stacey."

Doctor Brown craned her neck slightly, caught Girard's eyes. He saw her knuckles turn white as she clenched the notebook she held tightly against the mounds on her chest. It was undeniable that she was attractive—she was tall and thin with curves in all the right places, and she had a face that turned heads—but Girard did not care about that. She was nice to look at, especially when her bangs fell in front of her eyeglasses without her noticing when she concentrated, or when she chewed on the cap to her pen while she listened to what Girard had to say, or when she pressed her shoulder blades together and crossed her arms as if she were comforting herself when Girard would break down; it was in those moments Girard knew Doctor Brown genuinely sympathized with him as opposed to feeling sorry for him simply because he was her patient—the difference between the two was easy to spot. But despite her obvious attractiveness, Girard had romantic eyes for only one woman, and nothing would change that—not even death.

"I'm sorry, Stacey," Doctor Brown said as she turned back to her, "but unless Girard authorizes you to join in for our session, I'm going to have to ask you to wait in the lobby."

Girard felt their eyes on him.

"Dad?" Stacey said.

He cringed.

"I think it would be nice if I sat in," Stacey said. "So that I know how to better support you in case something like this happens again."

Girard looked from Stacey to Doctor Brown, whose eyebrows rose as she looked at him. He wondered if she had seen the news report about Miriam.

"I . . ." Girard tried. He could not find the words to finish.

"I think it's best if you wait out here," Doctor Brown said, hardening her voice just enough to make an impact.

Stacey kept her focus on Girard, blinking only occasionally. After a long few seconds, Girard nodded, and a sense of relief rushed over him. Stacey's shoulders dipped and her face sunk, but she tried to offer her best smile anyway. She nodded and turned back down the corridor, did not protest further.

"Thank you," Girard whispered to Doctor Brown.

"Come on in," she said as she rested a gentle hand on his shoulder and lead him across the threshold to her office. "Tell me what's going on."

CHAPTER TWELVE

After talking for an hour in Doctor Brown's office, Girard had nothing to say on the ride home. As much as he disliked Stacey's unwelcomed intrusion on his life, the reality was he was appreciative of her. More than that, he needed her right now. If for nothing else, her car made his life easier and saved him a long walk into town. The last time he saw the only vehicle he and Miriam shared was when it was at the bottom of the ravine off Highway 15. Where it was taken after that, he was not privy to. He imagined he would be without for some time. But more than that, it was nice to have someone else around, even if it meant revisiting old heartache.

"Thanks for being here," he said as Stacey pulled into the drive.

She stopped the car, yanked on the parking brake, and unclicked her seatbelt. Only then did she acknowledge what Girard said, and that was by shooting him a menacing glance that doubted his sincerity. Girard meant what he said, but he saw no reason to try to justify himself.

"I need a drink," Stacey mumbled as she slid out of the car and slammed the door.

Girard sat alone and watched Stacey walk away. Emptiness filled his soul. When she disappeared into the house, he got out and headed directly for the green house. The morning had come and gone, and he was behind schedule yet again. Thursdays were for red flowers, and the amaryllis waited.

The thing about the amaryllis, what made it unique, was its shape. Florists commonly said its petals looked like a trumpet, the way they curled at the edges and formed a tunnel at the mouth. Girard was not so sure about that. He saw the center of the amaryllis as more of a black hole with banks that would inevitably cave in, yet never seemed to. Or maybe that was a metaphor for Girard's life, a way to symbolize the nightmare that was his existence. Either way, the irony was striking. Whether the amaryllis was a floral representation of Girard's life, or if it was the trumpet of the garden, it had a profound impact.

The amaryllis was Miriam's favorite flower of the week. It was partially because of the color—the way the blood-red petals would sometimes get white stripes on them, or the way the brightness of it reminded her of the passion she had for life. And the trumpet aspect, Miriam took to heart. The amaryllis took charge of her garden, most prominent in its positioning—the leader of the pack. And while the black hole could be a metaphor for Girard's life, the trumpet could be the metaphor for Miriam's, and all she stood for. Miriam was a leader with a take charge mindset, certainly in their marriage, and so it made perfect sense why she appreciated the brilliance of the trumpet of the garden. Like with life itself, the appreciation of the flowers and their colors was all a matter of perspective.

Inside the living house, the cool stem freshly snipped firmly between his fingers, Girard switched out the marigold. The water in the vase was murky with broken pieces of the sepals that floated like buoys in a summer lake. Girard thought it looked unkempt, and he felt guilty about it, as if he let Miriam down. The freshness of the water was subpar, and it was all because of him. It had not been changed in over twenty-four hours. He hurried to the kitchen to remedy that.

A fresh sponge, near-scalding water, and a quarter's worth of dish soap took care of it. Girard scrubbed the vase until he saw his ugly reflection in it, then he refilled it with cold water from the tap. He felt better once the amaryllis was in its place on the center of the dining room table next to the acrylic watering can of sugar. He took a deep breath and a weight felt lifted. He pulled out a chair and sat, then exhaled hard.

Over his shoulder, Stacey entered the room. The temperature seemed to drop when she did, and Girard could tell something was wrong. He turned toward her, toward the cold, as she stood in the entryway.

"Where's the vodka?" she said, her eyes suddenly as sunken as her face.

Something twisted in Girard's gut. Stacey's look made sense now. He misinterpreted the signs on her face before—the deep bags under her eyes, the exhaustion behind them. The distress, as he saw it, was not from emotional pain or from being beaten down, but from something worse. Something much worse. Stacey was becoming him, from a different lifetime ago. Or maybe she already became him—he could not know for certain.

While it was true he knew nothing about her as an adult woman, he now felt like he knew her better than she knew herself. He had been through it—the struggle and the pain and the torment. The addiction. It destroyed his life. And now his daughter followed in his footsteps. As a father, it was his worst nightmare.

Stacey had an empty tumbler in her hand, which dangled angrily by her hip as if she might toss it. She drummed the glass with her nail. Girard stayed seated.

"Where'd you get the glass?" he said.

"Where's the vodka?"

Girard craned his neck, found a clock. "It's noon."

"And?"

"I don't have that stuff lying around anymore."

"Bullshit." Stacey left the room. Thrashing began right away.

Girard kept seated still, waited patiently, not bothered by the inevitable mess that was being made. He had been in her shoes before and could sympathize. He did not know bad she was, how far down the road to alcoholism she had fallen, how deeply indebted she was to the drink, but he knew what could happen. What he experienced was the worst-case scenario, at least to him. Some people had to learn life's brutal lessons the hard way, and he was one of them. While terrible, it also meant he knew how to react to Stacey.

Do nothing.

Trying to interrupt her onslaught would be worthless. Trying to talk rational sense into her would be a waste of breath. Getting angry would be fruitless. Girard knew those things because he had been through it, spent many long, lonely days trapped in the shadow of the helplessness. Miriam tried all those methods on him, none of which helped or stopped what happened, not even slowed it. He did not remember much, but Miriam later told him her efforts to fix him made him worse, more irate, pushed him further away from reason. Made him more obsessive. So she learned. She learned to let him wear himself out, to lash out, to thrash through the house as if he were a madman. It was the only thing that calmed him down.

Now, as he sat at the dining room table, his teeth clenched, he grimaced each time another piece of glass shattered on the other side of the wall, he understood what Miriam went through. What he put her through. It was a miracle she did not throw her hands up in surrender years ago. Miriam was a saint.

Girard was hurt, but not in the normal sense of the word that had become so foreign to him. At the moment, he was absent of physical pain, always the emotional, but there was something resembling sorrow present within him. It was sorrow for Miriam, for all she went through, for all he put her through. For Stacey, there was only pity. For himself, the guilt was unbearable.

When Stacey finished, the eerie silence returned. Then she appeared in the dining room, out of breath. Girard sat in the same position—his hands folded, legs crossed, shoulders hunched—and followed her with his eyes. She made her way around the table and sat next to him, left a chair in between, looking disheveled.

"How long has it been?" Girard asked.

Stacey dropped her head, shame rightfully coming to the forefront. "Couple years."

There were several ways Girard could respond, none of which seemed appropriate. So he settled on nothing, decided he would wait it out. They sat in silence for a bit.

"Have you gotten any help?"

Stacey sniffled, then lifted her wrist to her nose and wiped. When she looked up, her pupils were hidden behind puddles, surrounded by red vein-like streaks.

"Did you?"

"Eventually, yes. But not before it was too late."

"The accident?"

Girard looked away.

The accident. The worst day of his life. The day that changed everything.

"Can we talk about it?" Stacey said.

"No."

"I want to know, Dad. I feel like I have a right to know."

"You already know."

"Not everything."

"Everything you need to know."

"What happened that night?"

Girard exploded out of the chair as if he were shot from a cannon. His feet landed on the floor with a thud, the joints in his knees taking the brunt of his full body weight at once. They nearly buckled.

"Goddammit, I said I don't want to talk about it!"

Stacey got to her feet too, just as wobbly. "Can we please just talk about it?"

Girard brushed past her and stormed out of the room. His ears buzzed while he huffed. A tingle leaped onto the back of his neck. The living house's entire frame shook as he slammed the door and stepped outside.

#

Girard retreated to the green house. Where else? The door did not lock because there was not ever a need for it. There was nowhere else he could go, nowhere else he wanted to go. He needed to be alone.

He sat on the stone in front of Miriam's frog garden. Water flowed like a faucet from the happy frog's lips. The repeated dripping against the basin was one of the most soothing sounds in Girard's world, and it had the knack to settle him during some of his most anxious moments.

The assorted rainbow of flowers in Miriam's garden flourished. The reds, blues, and pinks were most distinct. The lighter ones were just soft enough to bring pleasure to the eye, yet dark enough so they would not disappear in the shadows of the others. The waterfall in Miriam's other garden was small but spectacular. The afternoon hit it exactly right through the glass panels above so that it sparkled. To Girard, this place was heaven on earth.

He settled. His anger from before dissipated. The knot in his chest loosened itself, the tension fell off. Before long, the conversation with Stacey was all but forgotten. The green house was a magical place.

With his eyes closed, Girard forced himself backward. He slid his legs forward, stretched out his torso, and sprawled out on the stone. It was cool through his shirt and on the exposed skin on his arms. But it was refreshing too. Between the coolness on his back and the warmth on his face that kept his eyes from opening, Girard felt centered in a way he had not in quite some time. His body felt as if it were floating, his mind free of all negativity. His thoughts went to where they usually did during unconsciousness—back to that stormy night thirty-seven years ago.

#

Girard was back in the car again. Miriam was at his side, her ruby lips wide with laughter. Conway Twitty serenaded them through the speakers. Miriam's expression quickly turned from bliss to terror as she grabbed onto his hand and squeezed, pinching so hard Girard thought she might puncture the skin or snap the bones underneath it.

Girard turned back to the road.

Behind the darkness were flurries that lit up like candelabras on fire from the headlights. They were alone in the night. The car spun as if it were a feather in a windstorm, and their world became unrecognizable in a haze of madness and uncertainty.

Miriam screamed. Genuine panic overtook her tone. The vibration of it made Girard's ears ring, the pressure so strong he thought his eardrums might burst.

Then there was a blast.

Metal exploded into metal. Glass shattered. Steel crunched. The airbags failed to deploy. Everything was hot.

If Girard blacked out, it was only momentarily. Because the next thing he knew, the car came to a stop against the guardrail, steam from underneath the hood floated toward the stars, and he was alive. His head pounded while his vision spun. He tasted blood on his tongue, felt the ache where he had bitten it. His sternum pulsated underneath where the seatbelt crossed. Everything was hazy.

Every part of Girard's body hurt. Blood caked his hand after he wiped his lips, and there was an unusual pressure behind his eyes. But he was okay. Wounded and dazed, probably concussed, but okay. He could not remember what happened to get to that point.

Conway Twitty was there. He kept singing, not affected by what just happened, hitting notes that Girard could only dream of. But that was only background noise. Girard tried to remember what happened, where he was, what he was doing. He struggled at first. But then it all started to return. Slowly. Then faster.

Miriam!

Girard knew it was bad. In his heart, he felt it. The cabin smelled different. Heaviness took Girard's breath away. A penetrating sensation tore into his chest. He just knew.

When he looked over at Miriam, it was just as bad as he expected. Blood was everywhere. The window next to her was shattered, and piles of glass covered Miriam's shoulder and waist. Her hair was disheveled. Her neck slouched forward, the belt across her lap the only thing that kept her from falling into the dashboard. Dark scarlet streaked down the side of her face from the impact. Her legs and stomach and neck were covered with it. Girard could not tell where it came from, but he expected the worst.

He reached across the transmission and touched the bare skin above Miriam's knee where her dress slid up. "Miriam?"

There was no response.

"Miriam? Miriam, are you okay?"

She did not move.

"Miriam?"

Panic set in. He fumbled with his seatbelt. His hand shook as he tried to unclip it.

"Miriam!"

The belt unclipped and swung over his shoulder, freed Girard to approach his wife. He leaned across her and grabbed her face between his hands and lifted her head up. His everything shook, both from the aftershock and the adrenaline within him that tried to break through.

Miriam's eyes were closed. Blood trickled from her ears, more from her lips.

Girard shook her again. "Miriam? Are you okay?"

She hunched motionlessly.

Was she dead?

It was hard to tell.

Girard felt for a pulse. He found one.

The impact of the crash was incredible. Miriam got the worst of it, the passenger's side taking the brunt of the guardrail's resistance. Girard could not understand why he was mostly unscathed.

Miriam saw it coming before he did. Her reaction time was a tick sharper than his that night. That was not enough to make the difference, though, was it?

No way. Not a chance.

Or was it?

Girard tried not to think about it. He had a drink or two, but he was not lubricated, not by any means. Miriam would have told him so if she thought he was unfit to drive, right? Definitely.

No, no, no.

Girard shook his wife again. "Miriam? Please wake up. Please!"

But she did not. Not for a while. Not in time.

Girard threw his face in his hands and screamed until his lungs hurt. Somewhere in the background, Conway Twitty wrapped up his harmonies through the crackling of the speakers.

What a shame, what a sight. A good love died tonight.

He had no idea how right he was.

#

Girard woke covered in perspiration, his heart hammering in his chest. The stone beneath his back boiled from his heat. He immediately reached for his face, expected blood, but found only the indent above his lip that permanently scarred him and reminded him every day of that night, of where it came from. The visions were so vivid, so disturbing, so precise. Girard thought he might be sick.

On the other side of the green house, the door opened. Light from the outside world shone inside—more light than was normal. The door stayed open longer than it should have.

"Hey! Who's there?" Girard said. "Close the door."

He struggled to his feet. His whole body trembled from his dream. By the time he regained his composure and was able to stand, he was angry. The door to the green house remained ajar, threatening to taint everything he worked so hard to preserve. Girard was convinced he already felt the temperature rising.

"Hey! Close the door!"

Stacey appeared. "What?"

"Close the goddamn door!"

"Why?"

"Now!"

Girard steamed. He had visions of the waterbeds drying out, of the soil hardening, of the flowers dying. He spent too much time ensuring the conditions were pristine for maximum growth inside the green house to let someone ruin it out of carelessness. Miriam's gardens, like Miriam herself, deserved the absolute best.

Stacey jogged back to the door and closed it. Girard ran toward her.

"What does the thermostat say?" he said. It was mounted to the wall next to the door.

Stacey read it. "76.4. Why?"

Girard exhaled. The damage was not permanent.

"Jesus Christ, Dad. What's wrong?"

Girard breathed heavily, pulled up. "Never leave that door open. Do you understand?"

"Fine, God."

"Do you understand?"

"I understand!"

"Good."

"My God, Dad. What's wrong with you?"

"These gardens are important to me."

"They're just flowers."

"Not to me. To me and your mother, they're extraordinary. I don't expect you to understand."

"Fine."

Girard put his hands on his hips and sucked wind. "Why are you in here? You shouldn't be in here."

"I didn't know. I was calling you from outside."

"What is it?"

"There's someone here to see you."

"Who is it?"

"Two men, I didn't catch their names."

Girard turned back to Miriam's frog garden and started that way. "Tell them I'm not here."

"They're cops."

Girard stopped.

Then he turned, met Stacey's gaze, and followed her back into the living house.

CHAPTER THIRTEEN

"Can we come in?" It was Sergeant Bell. He fingered the brim of his cap.

Girard scanned the men. He searched their faces for a glimpse of a miracle, for hope there was a giant mistake. But their faces were firm, as solid as stone. Sergeant Bell was difficult to read. His lips touched and his jaw clenched, as if he were underwater. His shoulders were strong and wide. His younger partner stood motionless a step behind him.

Girard stood to the side and pulled the door open wider. He sensed Stacey behind him. Anxious energy radiated from her. Girard's thoughts were foggy. The two officers brushed past him and took off for the living room as if they knew something Girard did not. He closed the door and followed. The three of them stood in a makeshift circle near the sofa, the awkwardness not as strong as it could have been. The walls smelled like Miriam.

"How are you holding up?" Sergeant Bell asked. His hat was still in his hands.

Girard shrugged.

Both officers nodded. What could they say? What could anyone say?

"The reason we're here," Sergeant Bell said, "is we have some news."

Girard perked up. But only a little. The flat expressions on the officers' faces told him it was not good news. He felt Stacey lurking around the corner.

"The coroner completed her examination of the . . . of Miriam's body. And . . . Mr. Remington, may I ask you a question?"

"Go ahead."

"Is, was your wife a heavy drinker?"

Was.

Girard felt his face flush. His skin began to boil through the heat of his anger, which rose quickly. "No. Never."

"Never?"

"Never."

Sergeant Bell shot a glance at his partner and shifted his weight. "I don't mean to question you—"

"Then don't."

"It's just that the coroner ran a litany of tests on Miriam's body, including a forensic toxicology report, to find out what may have happened to your wife. Which is not unusual. While it may appear obvious, considering the position and location of your vehicle, it's our duty to investigate all untimely deaths."

"What are you getting at?" Girard did not like that the sergeant was stalling. His skin warmed faster by the second, and he sensed an implosion coming on.

Sergeant Bell sighed. "This is difficult. I know you said Miriam was not a heavy drinker—"

"She's not!" Girard caught himself, realized he referred to her in the present tense. And based on the cringe that crawled over the younger officer's face, Girard knew he heard it too. But Girard was not about to correct himself. To him, there was still a sliver of hope left.

"The toxicology report calculated her blood alcohol level at 0.12. That's almost double the legal limit."

"Impossible," Girard said. He tried to catch his breath as his chest hammered.

"I know it may be hard to believe right now, but sometimes we don't know our loved ones as well as we think we do."

"Stop it."

"Mr. Remington—"

"Stop it, right now! You didn't know Miriam."

Sergeant Bell opened his mouth, about to say something, but stopped.

Girard crossed the room and escaped into the dining room. He slid around the eight empty chairs and past the lonely table, through the vortex and assortment of vibrant fruits that hung on the wall, and threw himself toward the corner cabinet. The glass front stared at him with dying temptation, the useless china a dull shimmer. He dropped to his knees as his hands trembled and pulled open the cabinet. Tumblers and shot glasses and shooters sat—rows and rows of them of, each of varying shapes, sizes, and designs. There were no bottles.

He slipped into the kitchen, yanked open the refrigerator doors so hard the entire unit screeched forward on its wheels. He rummaged through the chill—looked behind the milk, under the head of lettuce, inside the fruit and vegetable drawers; he slid half-empty bottles of ketchup and tomato sauce and jarred cranberries to the side; he opened the lid of the egg carton. There was no wine, no vodka, no whiskey or bourbon. No nips or moonshine or scotch or gin or rum. No pale ales or IPAs or watered-down light beers. Not a drop.

He slammed the doors closed.

Hidden in between the edge of the counter and the side of the fridge was a step stool—Girard wrapped his fingers around the foam at the top of it and pulled it out, fought to unfold it. By now, Stacey stood in the doorframe at his back, repeated his name softly. He heard the officers' boots clanking, felt their presence too close to him. Girard climbed the short steps until his knees were as tall as the counter. His joints shook as he outstretched his arms and began to whip open cabinet doors. Beyond the porcelain dinner plates and salad plates and bowls and serving trays was nothing, and neither was there above the cabinets where a wooden lip could easily hide a lying down bottle. Girard scooted over and slid his palm across the top of the fridge, and all he came back with was dust.

As he said, it was impossible.

Miriam did not drink. Not ever. Not anymore. Not in nearly forty years.

Girard dropped to the floor, his feet sprawled out in front of him as if he were a reptile. He pressed his back against the cabinet door and tried to catch his breath. He was exhausted. When he turned and reached for the knob, Stacey stopped him.

"Stop, Dad," she said. "We get it."

Girard let his arm fall, then his head. He wanted to cry but could not. He wanted to weep like a child, like a fussy newborn. He wanted the tears to roll down his cheeks and cool his skin, singeing from the heat underneath. More than ever, he wanted the pain to stop. He needed it to. He was desperate.

"Let me help you." It was Sergeant Bell again.

Girard looked up, the weight of his head like a bowling ball on his neck, and saw the sergeant's outstretched hand reach toward him. Girard met his eyes. A hint of sympathy lingered behind them, a flicker of sorrow.

"I'm sorry," Sergeant Bell said. "It was inappropriate to bring it up like this."

Girard took his hand. While clammy, his grip was like a vise. In his soul, Girard felt the sergeant's steady presence, and he found a bit of relief. While the man was naturally skeptical because of his profession, Girard sensed there was a softness to him, that he was empathetic at his core as a human being and a man. And that was just what Girard needed at the moment—to be around someone with that personal quality. While he could not ignore the accusation he made, Girard put it out of his mind and gave himself to the will of the man before him as he was steadied to his feet.

"Let's go sit," Sergeant Bell said. He led Girard back to the living room.

Girard sat with a thump onto the sofa. Its cushions were infrequently sat on and firmer than he typically preferred, but the relief felt so good. If he closed his eyes, he could fall asleep in an instant.

"I'm sorry," Sergeant Bell repeated.

Girard waved him off. "Nonsense. You're just doing your job."

"Thank you."

"What else can you tell me?"

"Well, after the vehicle was exhumed and taken into police custody, we had a team go through it, looking for anything that might help verify Miriam's identity."

"And?"

Sergeant Bell turned and motioned to his partner, who retrieved his phone from his hip pocket and walked toward him. Sergeant Bell took it and carried it toward Girard, illuminated the screen in his face.

"Do you recognize this?"

Girard leaned forward. On the phone was a sharp-looking photo of a severely burned handbag. The long strap was charred and torn, the leather on the outside mostly black. One of the buttons was missing.

Girard's stomach churned, and he nearly retched.

While impossible to identify the bag in the photo, there was no denying Miriam had one of the same style. The color was different now—the one she carried for as long as Girard could remember was gray—but that made sense.

Miriam's handbag had been missing a button for a month or two now. Neither one of them had gotten around to sewing it back on, for whatever reason. He knew right where it was, collecting dust in the junk drawer in the kitchen. He felt defeated.

"It's hers," Girard said.

The officers looked at one another quickly, then back to Girard.

"Are you sure?" Sergeant Bell said.

"There's a button missing. We have it in the drawer." Girard dropped his head and sighed.

Silence fell.

"Can I see it?" Girard asked. He felt all six eyes in the room flick toward him, as if there were an electromagnetic field overpowering them. He was the magnet.

"The bag?" Sergeant Bell said.

"The car."

"I'm sorry, but I can't let you do that. The vehicle is in police custody until the case is closed."

"Can't I just look at it? Maybe there's something in there I can point out that could help."

"I'm sorry, Girard. I can't. Allowing you to see the exhumation was even unorthodox."

He called him Girard. Girard noticed. He looked up. Sergeant Bell was genuinely sorry—that much Girard could tell. The man was doing his best, and Girard felt guilty for trying to pressure him into blurring the line between right and wrong. But what could he do? It was his life.

"I'm terribly sorry," Sergeant Bell said.

Their eyes met, and Girard nodded.

"Listen, if there's anything you need, any support or guidance or anything, we have resources."

"I appreciate that."

Sergeant Bell nodded. Finally, he put his cap on, wiggled it just a bit until he was satisfied with the fit. He motioned to Officer Chatham, who left the room.

"I understand this is a difficult time for you," he said, "but everything is aligning from our end for a quick resolution to Miriam's case."

Girard craned his neck. He struggled to comprehend what Sergeant Bell implied.

"At this time, based on everything we know, I feel confident in encouraging you to begin making funeral arrangements. It's the only way to start moving on. It starts with closure."

He made it sound so easy, so simple.

"Don't hesitate to call if you need anything. I'll show myself out."

And he did.

CHAPTER FOURTEEN

Girard sat in silence after the front door closed. He tried to process everything.

Were they right? Was it over?

He considered everything—Miriam's wedding ring, her purse, the Buick. It all certainly made sense, even to his skeptical mind. But without being able to identify her body, could he ever move on? He was not sure. Everything was still so fresh.

The toxicology report bothered him. There had to have been some sort of mistake. Could it have been that simple? That it was just a mistake. Girard did not know a lot about the process, but it seemed unlikely when he considered the importance of it all. But these technicians were just people too—imperfect, occasionally distracted human beings that made mistakes— and Girard, better than almost anyone, knew slipups happened. It did not make them bad people. Everyone deserved to catch a break sometimes, to get a second chance.

So Girard was not going to make a big deal about it. He could demand them rerun the toxicology test and make a stink until they did. But what would that solve? He knew the truth. Miriam would not have been drinking. It was not a part of their lives anymore. It had caused so much irreversible damage already that it was not worth it—that was how she felt about it. She was the one to pressure Girard into following her lead. It was her idea to stop.

Girard leaned back on the sofa and closed his eyes.

What now?

That was the question, was it not? What would he do now?

"Dad?"

Girard opened his eyes and leaned forward. Stacey sat across from him, her eyes watery, her cheeks wet. He did not know what to say. If Stacey wanted comforting, she was looking in the wrong place—he was not in any position to offer such; he could hardly comfort himself. He teetered on the edge of a breakdown—he felt it. Too much pressure might break him, and too much emotional stress could send him in a rapid downward spiral. He knew he needed to see Doctor Brown again soon, maybe even tomorrow.

"Daddy?"

"Don't. Seriously, don't."

"Don't what?"

"Don't call me that. You're almost fifty years old for God's sake." He sat up, pushed himself to his feet.

"You'll always be my dad."

"Stop it! You're a stranger! You haven't been around in how many years now?"

Stacey stood up too. "But I'm here now." Her voice was gentle, as if she were talking to a child. "We're going to need each other. Family has to stick together during times like these."

Girard was angry. Furious. He stormed out of the living room, just as hot as earlier, maybe hotter. How dare she? Seriously, how fucking dare she? First showing up unannounced, then trying to intrude on his private session with Doctor Brown, now this? It took all Girard had to not throw her out.

The anger swirled so deeply it gave him vertigo, and he spun right along with it. He had to release it. The phone was plugged back in again—from when Stacey used it to call Doctor Brown—although Girard hardly cared. The phone was his victim. He wrapped his fist of fury around the cord, squeezed it until his fingers were red with hatred, and yanked it from the wall. The plastic tip snapped when he jerked it, and a sliver of it flew somewhere over his shoulder.

He grabbed the sides of the phone base with his hands and shook it, screamed gibberish at it. He shook and shook until his biceps burned, and he pulled the unit right off the wall, drywall screws and all. A cloud of dust formed a haze in front of his face, and his ears buzzed from the crash as he smashed the phone against the kitchen floor.

But he was not done.

The phone was one thing, but the TV was another. The news had already gotten wind of the story, and he knew how that industry worked—they would plant the toxicology report results in the headline and falsely lead people to inaccurate conclusions. They would poison Miriam's reputation with lies and overdramatized details to improve their ratings, and her memory would be forever tainted. Girard would not stand for that.

He thrashed back into the living room, past a frightened Stacey, and toward the only TV he and Miriam owned. He spared the tube the same fate as the kitchen phone, but he still reached around back, stretched his shoulder out as far as it would go, and yanked out every cord he could get his fingers on. The box from the cable company whirled to a stop, the illuminated light on the front faded to black. Then, without thinking, Girard sped out of the room again, pushed through the rubble in the kitchen, and walked out the back door. Slamming it closed behind him, he nearly ran into the green house, then threw himself on the stone floor and wept the driest of dry tears until he blacked out.

#

Girard remembered waking up next to Miriam and being freezing cold. The breath from his nose fogged up the windshield. Small icicles formed on his seatbelt. His head pounded. He was disoriented. The accident from the night before was only a blur in his memory, the recollection of it felt like a dream. It took him a few minutes to catch his bearings.

Next to him, Miriam was not conscious, but she was alive. He heard her breathing, saw her chest rise and fall with each breath. His seat vibrated each time she shivered. Girard reached for her, gently, as if she were a wounded canine, and shook her. There was no response. He called out her name and was disturbed by how raspy it sounded, how strained. How unwell.

The sun was still behind the mountainous horizon, but the glow above the tree line told Girard morning was not far away. The moon fell. Girard looked down and saw the keys hanging in the ignition still, unmoving. He reached for them. His muscles were frozen stiff and his fingertips were numb, but he eventually found the strength to grab on and twist. He tried once, twice, thrice, but the engine failed to turn over. The ignition clicked. Girard let go and reached overhead, flicked the switch on the light above the center console. No light. He flipped the headlights off then back on, pulled the lever to try the high beams. Still no lights. The backlight on the radio was black.

Aside from the cold, Girard was weak. His lips were cracked so badly they stung with every breath he took. His everything was sore. He needed help. Miriam needed help. The situation had become dire. As the memories flooded back to him like a tsunami in his mind, Girard found himself fixated on Miriam's seat. Frozen blood crusted the floor beneath it, although it hardly looked the part. It was more pink than red, and Girard was astounded at the quantity. His eyes crept upward—they started at Miriam's feet and ankles, her legs, her belly, and her chest; then to her neck and her mouth and nose and ears. Blood was everywhere. She was covered.

While he did not know the extent of her injuries, or if she would even survive, Girard closed his eyes and thanked the heavens. He did not consider himself to be a spiritual man, but he was not opposed to the possibility of something beyond his understanding, either. He turned to God when he needed something, or if he had no other options in the observable universe. Judge him if you may, but at least he admitted it. He thanked God for not killing her, for giving Girard a chance to fight for her, to fight with her. He thanked God for letting him live too. For why, he would soon learn. There was a little girl at home who needed him and Miriam around, and if for nothing else, it was his responsibility as her father to ensure she was taken care of.

But his mind was preoccupied with the moment. It felt significant.

When Girard's moment of earnest passed, he tried to get out of the car. His fingers were just loose enough to grab onto the door handle, and with the force of his entire body weight slammed against the door, he was sure the door would open. But it did not. The glass in his window was like a frozen puddle, a sheet of ice, a sure sign the snow had changed into rain overnight. Either the door was frozen shut, or there was some frame damage from the spinout. Or a combination of both. It would not budge.

Running on fumes, Girard firmed up his shoulder and swung his body back and forth until he had nothing left to give, until his entire left side pulsated. The door would not move an inch.

"God, please, God! Please help!"

He did not know what else to do. Tears welled up behind his eyes as he looked over to his wife again. He wondered how much time she had left before it would be all over. He feared nothing but the worst now. When God did not answer, Girard got angry. He balled his fingers into fists the best he could and took out his aggression on the steering wheel, then he threw his face onto it and sobbed. He sobbed like a helpless child, and that was exactly what he felt like. He felt worthless for letting his wife down and for not having the strength to save their family. He thought about Stacey and how she would cope. He thought about the vodka he had and wondered if that played a factor in what happened. The guilt was so strong he began to question why he was still alive at all.

Then he repented. He poured his heart out to God and asked for forgiveness, begged for it. He promised loyalty and commitment, and he swore he would kick the bad habits. He assured God he would be a better man.

It was not ten minutes later when a pair of headlights shined in the rearview, and he knew immediately God had answered him. He smiled and cried and was overwhelmed with joy and hope, because he knew, he just knew he and Miriam were going to be all right. And maybe, despite everything, it was not as bad as it seemed. Maybe he would be gifted a second chance after all. Maybe they all would.

CHAPTER FIFTEEN: Friday

Blue was depth. It was a deep emotional understanding and willingness to accept the faults of others, to trust their motivations, to withhold judgment. It was showing loyalty when others would not, could not, or should not, and to forgive even when forgiveness was unworthy. It was mastering the significance of a lover's union, always sticking by the other, even in the most difficult of times. It was downplaying a quarrel in favor of the good of the unification. It was remembering where it all began, and where it would ultimately end up. It was exhibiting selflessness, always.

Girard awoke on the stone floor with a neck so stiff his head could not move. It scared him at first. Physically, he felt trapped, paralyzed to some extent. While he knew calling out for Miriam would be useless, she was the first thought he had. But he quickly remembered how his life was different now, how Miriam would no longer be there to help him during times like these. It was a rude reminder he was alone now, that he would somehow have to navigate through his daily life without her. That was a foreign concept to him—Miriam had been by his side for more than four decades. It was a depressing reality.

Minutes passed—maybe only nine or ten, but definitely more than five. Girard lay flat on his back with his eyes admiring the sun that always seemed to shine first thing in the morning. He thought about it and could not recall the last time it rained. Thankfully, it made no difference to Miriam's gardens—the sprinklers were on a timer.

The flowing waterfall offered peace. Girard inhaled through his nose until his chest was full, held it, and pushed it through his mouth—it was a trick Doctor Brown taught him. He repeated it thrice. What it did was cleanse his mind and body of all the toxins that poisoned it. The best part was he could do it as many times as he needed or wanted in a given day and no one would think twice about it. Not as if he cared what other people thought about him, because he did not. Just Miriam.

Girard's neck slowly loosened up. His stomach growled when he sat up, and his vision blurred as his eyes adjusted. As much as his body felt as if he had been mauled by a semi, his psyche was in a good place, his mind maybe even sharp. The reality of the day hit him, and he accepted it. Between all the circumstantial evidence the police gathered about the accident, it was hard to disagree that everything pointed to the Jane Doe being Miriam. Girard wished he knew for certain but tried to accept he may not ever.

While the red bulbs of the Thursday amaryllis were Miriam's favorite, Girard had his: the hydrangea. That was Friday's pick. Not only was a fully bloomed hydrangea the most beautiful, natural bouquet in the garden, but the astonishing shade of blue was unlike any other in nature. Nowhere had Girard seen that shade aside from in a hydrangea garden, and for that, Girard could not help but stare in sheer amazement each time he saw one. He could not help but be uplifted in its presence.

He clipped one from Miriam's frog garden and carried it into the house.

Stacey was up, flipping eggs in a frying pan on the stovetop. She turned her head when Girard walked in, offered up a half-hearted smile, and kept flipping. Girard paid her no mind, moving in and out of the kitchen, doing what he had to do to switch out the flower in the vase.

"Excuse me," he said as he held a dripping amaryllis by the stem.

Stacey stepped aside but kept one arm extended over the frying pan, the spatula caked with partially cooked egg. Hidden underneath the counter was the garbage bin, and Girard tossed the expired amaryllis on top. The marigold and rose from prior days were browning. There was nothing quite like a freshly picked flower each day to show someone how much they meant to you. That was the least he could do for Miriam.

Girard left the kitchen and retreated to the dining room. He sat in his usual spot and turned his chair toward Miriam's as if she sat there next to him. As heartbreaking as it was, to Girard, it was the only thing that felt right. Anything less would dim Miriam's memory, which was not something he would ever do, not while he had control over it. He did have to stop himself from reaching out for her hand, though. He felt naked without her. Loneliness crept in like a bad dream.

The smell of fresh eggs hit his nose and reminded him of how hungry he was. His nose led his eyes to the doorway, where Stacey entered, a salad plate suspended above her fingers as if being delivered by a maître d'.

She sat on the opposite side of the table, across from where Miriam would usually be, where she should still be. "You hungry?"

Girard shook his head.

Stacey forked some, jammed it in her mouth. Girard's stomach twisted with jealousy.

"You do that every day?"

"Do what?"

"With the flowers. Swap them out."

He nodded. "Coming up on 35 years."

"Why?"

Girard held his position, looked at and admittedly through her. He did not want to tell her. And he could not understand why she would even want to know.

"I'm not criticizing," she said, as if reading his mind. "I think it's sweet. I wish Tom would do something romantic like that for me."

Tom was her husband. They had been married for a dozen years maybe, but Girard had only met the man twice. Tom was even more a stranger than Stacey.

"How is Tom?"

Stacey laughed. "I'm surprised you remembered his name."

Girard was not amused. But Stacey was right—Girard would not have known his name if she had not said it. Tom was a nobody. A faceless, nameless nobody.

"Tom's fine," Stacey said as she forked another bite. "He does his own thing and I do mine. After sixteen years together, there's not much to say to one another most days."

There was so much Girard wanted to say, so much he could say. Marriage was sacred. Two people mutually deciding to spend the rest of their years together was an amazing thing. But sadly, most people just went about their daily lives without truly being thankful for the gift they had right in front of them—the gift of true companionship and deep, devoted, everlasting love.

"But I don't want to talk about Tom," Stacey said. She put her head down and chewed.

Girard looked to where Miriam should be. Her smile, though sometimes sad, was enough to fill up his heart for days. And her touch, the way she rubbed her thumb over his index finger while they made company over coffee, warmed his soul. The taste of her lips, while not as sweet as they once were so many years ago, was still the most familiar place in Girard's world. He caught a whiff of her perfume—the one he first bought her for her fiftieth birthday, the same one he bought every year since—and he could have sworn she sat beside him. But when he opened the eyes he did not realize were closed, Miriam was not there. Her seat was as empty as it was a moment ago, and all Girard could do was sigh. He missed his wife.

"I hope you don't mind," Stacey said, bringing him back, "but I called the funeral home in town and made an appointment for this morning."

Girard craned his neck to meet Stacey's eyes. The crick made him wince, but it passed. "How?" He thought about the phone from yesterday, about what he did to it. Then he realized it was no longer in pieces on the floor in the kitchen—he did not notice earlier. Which made sense. Stacey must have cleaned it up and put it back together.

Stacey reached inside her hip pocket and yanked out her cell phone, shook it for Girard to see. "Good thing for these puppies. Your landline is out of commission." She smiled and made a silly face, stuck her tongue out like she used to when she was a girl. Girard missed that version of her.

Girard recognized she was trying to cheer him up, to make him laugh or smile. But it was hopeless. Her efforts would go unrewarded, no matter how hard she tried. His stomach still made gurgling noises while he sat, and he was surprised Stacey could not hear. He was glad he was not alone. As much as he thought he wanted to be, having Stacey there was good for him. Being alone in the house with just his thoughts right now probably was not the best idea.

The thing was, he did not know how to tell her. He did not want to give false impressions that her ghosting he and Miriam for so long was water under the bridge now, because it was not—his hesitation to engage with her was stronger than ever; he questioned her motivations for being there. Yet, he was glad she was there. For whatever her reasons were, Girard felt a little better knowing there was still a part of Miriam around. Which, of course, led to the bigger issue: Stacey would not stay forever, nor did he want her to. She had a life to go back to before long. She had Tom.

Girard did the best thing he could think to do. He did not try to smile at her, for he knew she would see right through it—anyone would. And it felt wrong to smile so soon, maybe not ever again. Or at least not for quite a while. So he got up from the seat, pushed it back under the table and said to Stacey, "Thank you for calling." Then he started to leave.

"Where are you going?" she called after him.

"Upstairs to clean up and get changed. When you finish here, I suggest you do the same. We're leaving in one hour."

CHAPTER SIXTEEN

Of the number of funeral homes in Helena, the one he and Miriam picked out for themselves was ten miles from their house. They had history there. Somehow Stacey knew and chose the correct one. It helped that the others were on the far side of town. Their appointment was not for over an hour, but Girard insisted on waiting. He wore his Sunday best, complete with a full tailored suit and necktie, though the waist was a bit snugger than the last time he wore it, even on an empty stomach. Stacey was not dressed the part.

The funeral director's name was Jay. Jay, what? Did it matter? Not to Girard. Talking with Jay was simply a formality.

Miriam had planned out everything about their deaths many years ago, everything from the type of commemoration service to the method of disposal to the final resting place—it was all laid out, for them both. It was just a matter of communicating it to Jay.

This is what would happen. Should Girard outlast Miriam, her wishes were simple: A quick cremation with no major service, and the final resting spot of her cremains was to be predetermined before her death—Girard knew the spot. That was it. It was something they reviewed annually once they hit sixty. Too young maybe, but Miriam was a planner, and she thought it was their responsibility to ensure their wishes were carried out exactly as they wanted. It was just the two of them, after all.

Why cremation? It was not much of a debate. Burying cremains would mean eternal unification with nature. It would mean the chance to be reincarnated as one of the plants they both loved so much. Even with a low probability of success, the chance would be granted annually during bloom season since cremains did not decompose. For Miriam, that would mean decades or centuries or millenniums, if it took that long, of attempts at, every spring, blooming into a blood-red amaryllis. It was her final wish, her eternal hope, to somehow be reborn as the flower she adored in the physical world. Girard loved her perspective on it.

Jay's Funeral Home and Crematorium—not so cleverly named after its director—had the role of arranging the cremation and completing and filing the death certificate. That was all. Girard confidently told Jay all about it.

Jay took notes and nodded occasionally to keep Girard talking. The desk between them was cherry mahogany with a glossy surface finish and too many accessories on top—an engraved gold pen stuck out of a special casing; a personalized clock ticked; a sterling silver ashtray collected dust. Girard wondered if that was either a twisted joke by an insensitive relative, or if the man was a smoker. But who was Girard to judge?

Most disturbingly, and entirely distasteful and inappropriate, was a dual fold hinged photo frame. On the left was a sunny photo of a pair of young girls—young being roughly ten- or twelve-years-old—and on the right, a clichéd snapshot of the same two girls along with Jay and another woman around his age. Girard found it unforgivable.

What was distasteful about that? The man had photos of his family on his desk at work—not unusual. It was not the photos themselves that bothered Girard, but rather the positioning of the frame. It could have been an honest mistake—maybe the frame was nudged outward by the overnight cleaning crew, or perhaps Jay knocked it with his yellow pad when he rearranged the top of his desk. But either way, with the frame tilted just enough so Girard could clearly make out the faces of those behind the glass, he could have walked out. And he may have, had it not been Miriam's precise wishes to make the arrangements as soon as possible, at this specific parlor. He understood it.

Still not understanding? It was a funeral home. The only reason there were visitors was to either plan for a future death or to make arrangements for the recently deceased. Families were breaking up. Widowers, like Girard, were going to be alone for maybe the first time in their lives. Widows were about to be without the support they always relied upon. Lives were being destroyed. And with Jay showing off his young, happy, lively family for all to see, Girard took it as a slap in the face. He could not stop himself from thinking negative thoughts.

To Girard's liking, they soon wrapped up in Jay's office. To say there were hidden rooms beneath the funeral home would not be entirely accurate, but it would not be inaccurate either. It was only hidden to the public, who stayed upstairs in one of the two mourning rooms, separated for privacy by only a flimsy sheet of drywall. But once an outsider inquired about becoming a client, a new section of the facility became available, and it was awful.

Jay led them behind the mourning rooms, where a shallow corridor with dim lighting and no ventilation swallowed them. At the end of the corridor was a secured door, accessible by password only. Jay asked Girard and Stacey to turn away, which they did. He pulled the door open and descended the stairs that lead belowground, and the heat blasted through the opening like the backfire of an engine. The heat whipped against Girard's face, pushed him back on his heels. Sweat immediately beaded on his face and neck and irritated the skin under his stubble. He stepped forward, peered down the wooden stairs, wondered if they led to Hell. Despite his instincts telling him not to, he followed Jay down. Stacey was at his heels.

As it turned out, it was not Hell at the bottom, although it may as well have been. There were two additional rooms, one labeled with an engraved plaque on the outside, warning intruders not to enter. Without inquiring, Girard knew what the room was for. The thought made his stomach twist. A furnace blasted on the other side of the door, and Girard pleaded for the door to be strong enough to entrap the heat, and the smell. It was eerie, being near one. Girard knew what was happening on the other side, and he could not help but think that Miriam would soon be in there. The idea of her being shut in a box and pushed into a furnace to be turned into ash made him woozy. But it was what she wanted.

His vision blurred. His chest thumped with intensity, caused him to sweat even more. Everything around him spun. The next thing he knew, there were forearms underneath his armpits, and he was assisted inside the second room. He plopped onto an upholstered armchair and felt all the strength being sucked away from his body. His knees felt weak, trembling as he slouched. The muscles in his neck tightened as they struggled to keep his head upright. His shoulders drooped. Breathing was difficult.

"Are you alright, Mr. Remington?" It was a man's voice.

Girard was not all right. He forced his eyes closed and waited for it to pass. Eventually, it did.

It scared him. This was not the first time a panic attack had rendered him physically incapable, powerless to the anxiety that ripped through his body. He recognized how often it happened lately but did not know what to do about it. How would he manage without Miriam?

"Are you alright, Mr. Remington?" The man repeated. By now, Girard was cognizant enough to recognize the man as Jay, and that made sense. Stacey stood next to him, her eyes wide like a bug's. Both of them breathed heavier than normal, their chests noticeably bouncing up and down as they stood.

Girard wrapped his fingers around the arms of the chair, felt soothed by the coolness of the wood, and pushed himself up straight. For as deathly hot as the stairs and lower corridor were, the room he was in now was the complete opposite. Air vents on the ceiling blew chilly air downward and cooled Girard from the head down. As time passed, his body slowly returned to full strength, replenished from within. He leaned forward, put his elbows on his knees, and looked around.

Before him was a wide, clean, and very bright room. Lights were everywhere, the ones overhead the brightest. Lining the perimeter of the room were long, wooden boxes—some half-closed, others fully open, some fully closed. Some rested on built-in wall shelves, others were propped up on rolling tables, featured as if on special. Girard pushed himself to his feet, took a second to catch his breath, and walked toward the wall closest to him.

The number of exterior colors—everything from cherry to golden brown, from pine to metallic gray to black—and styles were astonishing. The lid hardware could be sterling silver or pure gold or granite. The interior lining could be taffeta or velvet or satin or chiffon of any color or pattern in existence. There were different box thicknesses and lengths and widths to choose from. It was the most ominous place he had ever been to.

Girard felt a hand on his shoulder and almost jumped out of his skin.

"Mr. Remington?" Jay quickly pulled his hand away as if he had touched a hot stove. "Are you alright?"

"Should I call that doctor again?" Stacey said as she approached him.

"I'm fine."

"Dad, are you—"

"I'm fine."

They pressed him no further.

Girard explored the room. While he realized Miriam would be burned in one of the basic death boxes, it would not be her final resting spot, so he needed something perfect. She would stay with Girard forever.

He found what he was after on the other side of the wall that cut the room in half, lined up like prisoners on wall shelves from knee-high to the ceiling. Hundreds of them. Much like the casket choices, there was an abundance of urns, enough to satisfy the need for any style, shape, color, pattern, or material. Girard scanned the wall, quickly shifted his eyes up and down, left to right, until one captured his attention. It overwhelmed him at first, the immense pressure he felt to find a container suitable enough to hold the cremains of his dear wife. But some things in life just had to be done. Sometimes difficult, uncomfortable choices had to be made. And this was the worst decision imaginable.

But there it was on the shelf in front of him, directly in his line of sight. His eyes latched onto it and would not let go. It spoke to him, illuminated in the reflection of the recessed lighting as if it were spotlighted exclusively for him. All the others that surrounded it blurred as if insignificant or non-existent. It was like the feeling first-timers had when they walked into their dream house, or the way Girard felt when he caught Miriam's eyes on the street all those years ago. The choice was clear, the decision all but made for him.

Girard stepped straight ahead, right toward it, and outstretched his arms neck-high. He wrapped his fingers around it and held it in his hands, squeezed tightly, determined. It was cold and ceramic, and bumps crawled out of his skin when he touched it. He pulled the vase toward him and cradled it as if Miriam was already inside. He shut his eyes and rocked with it.

It was perfect.

Shaped like a flower and painted white with red swirls on the sides, it looked just like an amaryllis—Miriam's favorite. It was as if it were a sign sent to Girard to tell him this was it, that it was final, that it was over. That Miriam was gone. It hurt like hell, but Girard knew he had to learn to accept it and to try to move on. His wife was dead.

"A fine choice," Jay said.

Girard opened his eyes and blinked the dryness from them. The right one stung just a bit, threatened to water. Jay stood next to him, his hands held firmly behind his back, and he smiled. Girard was perturbed.

How could the man smile at a time like this?

"Made of the finest ceramic, this—"

"I'll take it," Girard said. "This is the one Miriam would have chosen."

"Great." Jay's smile grew wider. "I'll take it and prepare the crematorium for your loved one's arrival. I promise we'll take great care of her."

Girard handed the vase over to smiley, though without want, and feared he might experience another breakdown where he stood.

CHAPTER SEVENTEEN

On the drive back, Girard used Stacey's phone to call Doctor Brown. She could see him immediately. When they arrived, Stacey found a spot close by and slid the car into park.

"Want me to wait here?" she said, her voice hushed. Girard could tell she was worried about him.

"No, go back to the house."

"I'll come and get you in an hour then."

"No."

"No?"

"I'll walk back."

"It's three miles."

"I need the exercise."

Stacey leaned back and sighed, justifiably unable to find the right thing to say.

"But thank you," Girard said. "I'll be fine."

Stacey nodded, dropped both hands on the steering wheel, and said nothing. Girard unbuckled and slid out.

Inside, Doctor Brown led him to her office in the back. They settled— he on a cracked leather sofa across from her, she in a cushioned armchair. A permanent indent sunk in the cushion where he always sat, the split leather creased, and he embraced the familiarity of it. Doctor Brown shook out her pen and scribbled on her notepad, then dropped the pad on her lap and slid her glasses above her face and rested them on her head. She gave Girard her complete attention, kept the pen in her hand to fidget.

"It happened again?" she said. Her voice was so soothing, Girard felt instantly relaxed. Whenever she spoke, he listened. He craved her approval and valued her opinion, and she had his complete respect.

"Yes."

"What triggered it?"

He told her.

"That's a difficult situation," she said. "It sounds like you handled it very well."

Girard looked away.

"How have you been sleeping? Since Miriam's accident."

"Sleeping through."

"Nightmares?"

"Same."

Doctor Brown nodded. She leaned back, twirled the pen through her fingers. Girard knew what would happen next. It happened all too many times before. She would sit in silence until he spoke again, until he fully engaged with her, until he opened up. She would say nothing for their entire session if she had to—a theory Girard had not tested, but one he knew without needing to experience it. He could not explain why, but even with the comfort he felt with Doctor Brown, he tended to shut down, to not be forthcoming with how he felt. It took her forcing him to lead the conversation most days.

"The one thing I want," Girard said, "more than anything I've ever wanted in this life, is to feel. I want to weep and mourn the death of Miriam."

"From what you told me last time, it sounds like you've been improving. Anger is an emotion too."

"That's true, I suppose. But it's not enough."

"I can understand that. It's one of the side effects of the medication."

"I don't like it. I'm tired of it."

"Do you think you need it?"

Girard stopped, thought about it, and nodded. He was at least honest with himself about that.

"Then we need to come up with alternative ways to cope."

"How?"

She crossed her legs, tucked the pen behind her ear. "Well, that depends. For someone like you, someone with your interest in learning and the natural world, I'd suggest spending more time in nature. Consider going outside the comfort zone of your green house. Explore the world. What about going on nature walks, or trying some outdoor meditation? Many people find nature to be therapeutic. It can help release endorphins naturally for some people. You may find that too."

"I don't know," Girard said without hesitation, without giving himself an honest chance to consider it.

"You're going through a challenging time, Girard. Especially now, self-care is critical."

Girard knew she was right.

"What's your long-term goal?" she asked. "With your health. What do you want to achieve?"

Put in those terms required some thought. Some real, in-depth self-evaluation. Where would he go now, without Miriam? What would he do? Most importantly, what did he want? Sometimes the simplest answer was the right one. And in this case, it was exactly that.

"All I want," he said, "is to be able to feel again."

\#

Girard walked home. What Stacey said earlier was not entirely accurate—it more like two and a half miles to home, not three. And he did want the exercise. More importantly, he needed to think. What would he do? What he had not expected was the rain. It came down hard and fast. And he was drenched, his suit sopped, all but ruined.

It was a long, dreadful, lonely walk. The sky darkened, the dreary clouds replaced the smiling sun. The streetlights zapped on. Headlights zoomed past. Windshield wipers squeaked. Rubber tires spat pooled up rain onto the sidewalk as they passed through. The temperature fell.

When fatigue crept in, Girard slipped inside the glass shelter of a bus stop and waited it out. He caught a glimpse of himself in the reflection of a car window as it waited at a stoplight, and he felt pathetic. There he was—a lonely, wet, miserable old man with nothing left to live for—too stubborn to accept a ride from the only person he had left in this world. He looked homeless, felt worthless. In some ways, he thought it might be better if he were—that way, Miriam's presence would stop lingering with every step he took. But he could never leave her garden, or the green house. He would rather die than abandon it.

And so he thought about it. Dying. He surveyed the street, waited for the biggest and fastest semi that came through, and watched it pass. The wind smacked against him. The rain darted the glass around him with icy pellets. His teeth chattered. He watched the semi carefully, calculated if it would kill him if he jumped in front of it. If should, if he timed it right. And he would have done it, he would have tried. There was no doubt in his mind about it. Aside from the burden it would have put on the unsuspecting truck driver—it would be cruel and unfair to destroy their life; Girard knew the pain firsthand, and it would not be right to pass it on to someone else—there was one thing that stopped him.

Miriam.

Her cremains would be ready tomorrow, and he had to be there to accept them. He had to ensure she would get a proper resting place inside the vase that chose him from the wall of hundreds. It was his responsibility to leave her cremains where they belonged, buried in her frog garden in the green house. If Girard did not do it, no one else would know why or where or how. Or when. Did he even know when? The timing was the hardest part, was it not? How long should he keep her for himself before sharing her with the earth? Was it fair to withhold her from her last wishes of having the chance to become a wondrous amaryllis? He wrestled with the answer.

So he decided not to leap in front of the semi, at least not today. He had to stick around to see Miriam's wish through. But after that, all bets were off. He could struggle through one more day.

He stood. The fatigue had progressed beyond that, morphed into something closer to exhaustion. Home was a mile out. The rain came in sideways, drilled into his skin like shrapnel. He shivered. Headlights came and went, blew past him as if he were invisible, which was fitting. His life without Miriam was nothing, meant nothing. In many ways, he was an invisible mouth to feed, and not much else. The burden on society was greater than his contribution, and no one could tell him otherwise. He lacked purpose.

More headlights approached from behind. Girard's steps were short and slow as his muscles ached, and he was not sure he could make it home before succumbing to the tiredness. But he tried. What other choice did he have? Through the pattering of the pellets on the pavement, he thought he heard something. He stopped and turned, nearly stumbled, to look, but was blinded by headlights. A parked car sat near the sidewalk, only feet from him, and their lights shined directly on him. Girard lifted a hand and shielded his eyes but saw nothing beyond the whiteness. So he turned back and kept onward.

Then he heard it again.

A voice. Not in his imagination, but an actual voice, from a real person. He stopped again and listened hard through the rain and the howling wind, tried to comprehend what was being said. Then it came in clear.

"Wait!" The voice said, a woman's. "Hold on!"

The voice was unrecognizable in the conditions, but Girard welcomed the excuse to stop for a minute. He stood in the rain and allowed himself to rest, to catch his wind, and waited for the voice to come closer.

"There you are," the woman said as she rushed toward him. "I've been looking all over for you."

Stacey stood in front of him. Rain poured off her shoulders like a waterfall.

"What are you doing here?" Girard said. "I told you I'd be fine."

"You don't look fine."

Girard said nothing.

"Come on, let's get you home."

CHAPTER EIGHTEEN

As much as it wounded his pride, Girard allowed Stacey to help him get undressed. His suit stuck to him like glue, and it took them both to unpeel it from his body. It was the only good suit he owned, which made him anxious about tomorrow.

"We'll figure it out," Stacey said.

He believed her.

Girard rinsed off in the shower, let the warmth of the steam replenish the cold wrinkles on his skin with life. After he toweled off and changed into something warm, he met Stacey downstairs. She had said she wanted to talk.

A steaming mug of coffee waited for him on the dining room table, along with a salad plate's worth of crackers. The grounds in the mug smelled wonderful, warmed his palate. His stomach growled and begged him to give it fuel, which was something he had not done well enough lately. He knew that. But he did not care, either. He held the mug between his hands and sipped it. His tongue warmed, then his throat. A cracker made its way between his lips.

"Glad to see you're eating," Stacey said. She had changed too and now wore an oversized sweatshirt and bottoms that stretched at the waist.

Girard ate quickly, sipping coffee in between each bite.

"You're not well." It was a statement, not a question.

Girard swallowed and looked up at Stacey, sipped his coffee once more. "Neither are you."

She smiled. Or at least she tried. It was a sad smile, like the one someone may offer when they tried to be empathetic but were not sure what to say. "You're right."

Her admission surprised Girard. He was unsure of how to react.

"But you're worse," she said.

"My wife just died."

"She was my mother."

Touché.

"How bad?" she asked.

"I'm getting treatment."

"It doesn't look like it's helping."

"You wouldn't know. You're never—"

"I'm never around. I get it. You're right. And I'm sorry. But I can tell when my dad is not well."

Girard pushed the empty plate to the side, released the mug. He sighed. "I'm taking this medication, these antidepressants, and they make me numb."

Stacey squinted and pushed back from the table.

"Not physically, but emotionally. Which is worse. I don't feel emotions. Sadness, happiness, joy. I've had some angry outbursts, but I feel nothing during them. I can't control it. My entire world is numb. I feel so empty."

Stacey took it all in. She made a fist, pushed a knuckle into her mouth. "How long?"

"Years. I don't know how many anymore."

"Why don't you stop?"

"Can't. I need them. I can't even get out of bed without them."

Stacey stayed silent for a minute, processed her thoughts. Girard picked up the coffee mug, then put it right back down again.

"You know," Stacey said as she cleared her throat, "what I told you earlier about Tom. That's not entirely accurate."

Girard said nothing, waited for more.

"We're splitting up. We've been split up, actually. He moved out a year ago."

"I'm sorry."

"Yeah, well, who would blame him? I couldn't give him what he wanted."

"It goes both ways, you know."

Stacey laughed, but not for real. "That's what he told me. The truth is, he's a good man. A good husband. Supportive and romantic sometimes, and a good provider."

"What happened then?"

"What do you think? It was me. He was tired of coming home to a drunk every day."

Girard did not need validation, because he knew. But you never really know, even if you think you do.

"Three years ago, I had a miscarriage."

"I never knew that."

"What was I supposed to do? Call you up and say, 'Hey, Dad! Haven't talked to you in five years, how've you been? I was nine weeks pregnant but no longer am because I couldn't stop drinking. Okay, bye!'"—Stacey began to cry—"Tom never forgave me for it. Who could? I got sober for eighteen months after that, but we couldn't get pregnant again. We tried and tried and tried, but we couldn't. At my age, the doctor said it was unlikely anyway, so unless we wanted to try in vitro, it probably wasn't going to happen. But at that point, Tom had all but given up. He wouldn't even look at me anymore."

Girard's throat was so dry he thought he might not ever be able to swallow again. He did not know what to say.

"But you know who thought I was pretty?" Stacey smiled again, that same sad smile, through wet eyes. "Mr. Belvedere and Mr. Smirnoff and Mr. Grey."—she laughed—"I got myself my own little Christian Grey. Except he's a fucking goose!"

She threw her hands over her face and sobbed.

It explained a lot. The silence and the distance and the isolation. Stacey was so much like Girard it made him hate himself even more. Whatever bad genes he was given were transferred to her to continue the cycle. Always the bad ones. He got up and walked around the table, sat next to her. She smelled like nothing, absolutely nothing.

"It's ruined my life too," he said.

Stacey lifted her head and looked at him. "What?"

"And your mom's."

"The accident?"

He nodded.

Stacey sat up straight, slid a foot under her buttocks. "Will you tell me about it now? Please?"

Girard closed his eyes and thought about it, about the accident and the aftermath, about its impact on all their lives—he, Miriam, Stacey. There was so much Stacey did not know but should, especially now. He opened his eyes, found Stacey looking back at him, blinking, her sad eyes full of hope. At the moment, as he looked back at her, he decided it was time. The story had gone untold in its entirety for too long. Not even Doctor Brown knew everything. And now that he was the only person left on the planet who knew everything about that night thirty-seven years ago, it was time to share.

"Okay," he said. Then he sighed. "I'll tell you."

\#

The headlights that God sent that day saved Girard's life, and Miriam's. Their hero was just an ordinary man, a man with a shiny car with a phone attached to the center console. Not a common thing during those times. It was obvious the man was sent for them.

Girard did not catch his name. The man pulled up behind their car, managed to get Girard's door open, and called for help when he assessed the blood. He was remarkably calm, not a hint of panic in him. For all Girard knew, the man was a guardian angel, hand-picked and sent to rescue them. In the immediate aftermath, he was convinced of it.

When help arrived—first a pair of flashing reds and blues, then a bright red ladder truck, then an ambulance—the angel briefly chatted with an officer, then left. Girard caught the man's eyes before he drove away, and he swore he would never forget them. If he ever came upon the angel again—whether it be on earth or sometime in the afterlife—he would recognize him. And he would shake his hand and thank him. Certain eyes were unforgettable, the majestic type that demanded attention, the type that made people stop and stare—those were the kind of eyes the angel had. They were bluer than the ocean shining under a cloudless summer day, brighter than aqua gemstones, more addictive than methamphetamines. They complemented the dirt-colored blonde on his head, stood out against the black covering that hugged his neck. Girard wondered if it was possible the man was God himself, or if God was ever able to leave his throne at the pearly gates.

After the angel drove off into the sunrise and disappeared into the horizon, Girard did not remember much. Vaguely, he recalled being helped from the car and ushered into the back of an ambulance where he was wrapped in a blanket and had his injuries assessed by the EMTs. A second ambulance arrived on the scene for Miriam. It took the firefighters longer to remove Miriam from the car than it did Girard, and he felt anxious during the whole ordeal. He continued to pray to God, begged for Miriam to pull through. He hoped he would see the angel again, or some other sign that everything would be okay.

Before long, Girard and Miriam were in adjoining hospital rooms. Girard was still cold all over, but the feeling in his extremities returned. The doctor said he was lucky, that the worst he had was a mild case of frostnip and he would recover before long. Which he did. His arms and legs had deep bruises and lots of sore muscles and stiff joints, but he hardly noticed. He was more concerned about Miriam.

Despite asking to see his wife, or for them to share a room so he could keep watch over her, the doctors refused. All they told him initially was she was in bad shape. Unconscious, in a coma.

Within twenty-four hours, Girard was up and eating and using the bathroom and was thawed out. He had been discharged, but the furthest he made it was the room next door. Stacey was being watched after by her grandparents.

Miriam was tough to look at. Deep abrasions and multi-colored bruises covered her like giant freckles. Breathing tubes and feeding tubes and catheters poked and prodded her. Machines beeped. Green, digital charts moved up and down. Her eyes remained closed.

The chair Girard sat in was ordinary and clean but not comfortable. The wooden back pressed into his spine in a way that made him cringe if he leaned back too far, but he did not move from it. He sat there with Miriam's hand in his own, rubbed his thumb over the veins that ran like streams along her hand. He continued to pray to God, wished for the angel to return.

But then something happened that changed everything. Girard stopped praying, started questioning, stopped believing. Just like that. By now, Miriam's situation was apparent—between her physical assessment and the doctor's conversations with Girard. She was being monitored closely, checked every hour by one of the friendly but non-empathetic nurses. During one of the early afternoon checkups, Girard knew something was wrong. Seriously wrong. Life-changing wrong. The nurse's face fell white and her tone changed, and she refused to look Girard in the eyes. By the time she called for the doctor and the doctor arrived, Girard already knew. He knew in his heart the way parents sensed when their child was in danger, even without being in the same geographical location. He felt it.

The nurse and the doctor stepped out, left Girard by himself with Miriam inside the room. The hands on the clock moved slower than real-life ever truly did. He stood up and sat down, stood up and sat. He never strayed more than an arm's length from Miriam, ready to tend to her needs if she were to awaken. The worst kind of butterflies flew in laps in his gut.

When the doctor returned, Girard stood. The doctor asked him to sit, which he did, and he was hit with the news. The baby inside Miriam's belly was no longer alive, the heartbeat gone. Between the accident and the cold and the coma and the physical trauma, the baby was not strong enough to survive. The doctor was deeply sorry, and they arranged to have the baby removed later in the day.

The pain hurt so bad, Girard thought he would die. He wished it.

#

Stacey left for a while after Girard told her. To clear her head, she said. Girard wondered about her mental capacity to drive, but he did not mention it. Some things, he knew, were best left unsaid in certain circumstances. He had learned a lot throughout his life.

Girard could not blame Stacey for not wanting to talk about it, or for not being able to. Everything that happened to Miriam and their unborn baby had been his fault. If only he had not had the extra nip, or if he had just gone slower around the corner, or if he had gotten the car's tires changed like Miriam asked—that was something he left out. Weeks before, Miriam asked him to get the tires looked at before winter, but he had not gotten around to it. The reason? Laziness. That was it. It was on his to-do list, but he kept putting it off. There was never any indication the tire tread had anything to do with it, but he always wondered if it played a factor. Maybe the tread was worn too thin, and maybe that played a role on wet, slippery roads. Girard blamed himself every day. For everything.

Aside from Miriam and Doctor Brown and himself, Girard had never spoken of the accident to anyone before now. He entrusted Stacey with the information, although he did not know what she could possibly do with it to cause him any more psychological destruction than he had already put himself through. He was not sure why he told her. Did he regret it? It was an interesting question, one in which he considered. He leaned back and dropped his hands on the table, recognized how badly they trembled. He was surprised the food had not kicked in yet.

Did he trust Stacey? No, he did not. Did he feel better having spoken about the accident to someone other than his wife or his doctor? No, not particularly. But did he regret it? No. She deserved to know, did not she? Or maybe she did not. Girard was conflicted, his thoughts unclear, his mind lacked sharpness. His thoughts drowned within the torrent of confusion that flowed through his mind. Everything was a fog.

Throughout the chaos of the last couple of days, Girard realized he had not taken his medicine, and it all made sense—the fogginess, the jitters and the shakes, the angry outbursts. Those were all withdrawal side effects. Which also meant the breakthrough he thought he had perhaps had not been one at all, but rather just an effect of the discontinuation.

Damned if he did, damned if he did not.

But what did it matter at this point? What more did he have to live for anyhow? Tomorrow was Miriam's day, which was important. For that he had to be sharp, to be the best version of himself for Miriam. Beyond that, he had no clarity. And that was as far ahead as he could think about.

He got up, dropped his plate in the sink, and climbed the stairs. He popped his medication in his mouth and coughed it down with a small cup of water, then went into the bedroom and fell onto his bed. He thought not of Stacey or of Miriam, or of the green house or of the future beyond the next day to follow, but rather the darkness and the nothingness of the dreams that were bound to invade his mind.

CHAPTER NINETEEN: Saturday

Black was the morbidity of life. It was death and depression and sin. It was finality. It represented the eternity that would inevitably be everyone's destiny. It was the black hole most tried to avoid or ignore in life, knowing it was a battle that would eventually be lost. It was sorrow and despair, remembrance and mourning. It was sadness. It was never being able to forget, despite wanting nothing more than to. It was learning to live with yourself and your wrongs. It was the darkness within everyone.

He awoke at dawn. He slept well, long and deep. Dreamless. It was refreshing. The remnants of the rain from the night before remained, the clouds outside gray and gloomy. The driveway was black with stains. The tops of the trees closest to the sky danced. It felt like a funeral type of day.

Girard slid out of bed and showered and shaved and parted his hair to the left, then he hurried to cover the mirror back up so his eyes would not wander. He flicked a splash of aftershave on his neck, sprayed a pump of musk on his chest. In the bedroom, his raisin black suit hung from a metal hanger on the door, covered by a clear unbranded bag. He thought nothing of it initially, but then he remembered last night—the rain and the sopped suit. And he did not own a bag like that. Upon further inspection, the suit was unquestionably his—the same frayed bottom edge, the loose twine sticking out of the bottom left quadrant of the button at the top. It was the suit he wore the day before, except, impossibly, it was dry and cleaner than it had been in a long time. He unpacked it and dressed.

There were two explanations he produced as he descended the stairs, the heels of his wingtips clanking against the wood, but only one was reasonable. The first thought that came to his mind was the angel from the accident thirty-seven years ago, but he quickly dismissed it. He no longer believed in the possibility ever since the day at the hospital, and even if he did, that was not how those things worked. But he knew so little about those mythical ideas that he could not help but wonder if that actually was how those things worked, that maybe it was about more that than feelings or faith or hope. What if, like the cliché, mysterious and unexplained phenomena could happen?

Girard made it to the bottom and turned the corner, headed for the kitchen. Stacey was there, munching on a slice of toast over the sink, a spectacular thinning black dress draped over her. Her hair was bright and straightened and fell at her shoulders. She looked up when Girard walked in, though reactionless. Girard watched as she chewed, as the bones in her cheeks popped with each crunch. From the side, her chin leaned forward at the end and showed off how long her face was. In so many ways, she reminded Girard of a young and enthusiastic Miriam, before life happened. Stacey was beautiful.

Girard was sad to see Stacey like that, though he could not actually feel that way—it was a complicated experience to try to explain; any of them, really. His emotions. Doctor Brown seemed to understand, but she was the only one. His heart felt it—all the love and sadness and pain and grief—but his head did not. He knew within himself he was supposed to feel a certain way—or maybe it was that he once felt that way about a particular moment, were it to have happened at a different point in time—but the impact on his body was minimal, if it registered at all.

Confusing, right?

That was how he felt—confused daily, unsure what was real and what was not. Was he permanently hardened to emotion after all he had been through that he physically could not get to the point of outwardly expressing it anymore? Or was he incapable of expressing it because his brain was tranquilized because of the medication? Or was it a combination of both, or neither? It was a daily struggle as he tried to navigate through the minefield of his impotent brain. He was powerless over it and his thoughts, and it scared him every day. Miriam was what got him through. And now Stacey, who physically resembled her mother in the best of ways, under the worst of circumstances, reminded Girard yet again of all he had lost. His dearest wife, his Miriam, was gone forever.

"You found it," Stacey said.

Girard shook himself, tried to get back into the moment. He forced out a nod, but not much else. A nod was the best he could manage today.

"Found a boutique department store downtown. Turns out, instant dry cleaning is a thing. Did you know that was a thing? I didn't know that."

Annie's was the name of the shop she mentioned, Girard knew of it.

"I hope you don't mind. I grabbed your suit while you were sleeping."

"Thank you."

Stacey looked down at her bare wrist, then at the microwave. "I'll be outside when you're ready." Then she left the room.

Her cheeriness seemed off, out of place, inappropriate even. But what could Girard say to her? Everyone coped in their own way. It was almost 7:30 a.m. and Jay expected them whenever, he had said yesterday, and Miriam would be waiting.

Miriam.

By now, her body would be unrecognizable, burned to an ashy pile of gray cinders. Just awful. Cremation itself was awful, was it not? Burning a body until there was nothing left but ash, removing the bone fragments and foreign metals that would not disintegrate. But it was what Miriam wanted, Girard too one day, no matter how morbid the thought was. Everyone had their reasons for how they wanted to be laid to rest, Girard no exception.

It was time. Stacey was outside and the inevitable could not be pushed off forever. Soon it would all be over, and that would be that. Tomorrow would be a mystery, today a memory. Just another one of Girard's ugly, despicable memories. It was time to get his wife.

#

As promised, Jay awaited them with open arms—in the most literal sense, as he welcomed Girard and Stacey with a wide embrace. Girard let it happen. But that was it. Just once.

Jay ushered them inside, past the two mourning rooms, down the dark corridor, toward the door at the end. Girard followed in step as they descended into the underground. The furnace room was quiet, though the heaviness of the calm after the storm lingered. When they pushed into the adjacent room—the one with the wall of beautiful vases and a never-ending glut of death boxes—it was different than before. Girard's world stayed still, the vertigo kept at bay. Physically, he felt strong and capable and a million miles from where he was yesterday. Was he ready or adequately prepared or accepting of the situation? No, never. That was not it. Getting a grip on his thoughts and feelings, assessing their purposes and significances, was impossible. Often, he could not decipher why he felt the way he did, or why he did not. There was little explanation of the way he felt.

What was it?

Calm.

There was a calmness within him that leveled him. Where it came from, he could not know. Unexpected, it was. He amazed himself sometimes with where his thoughts went and where they came from, and how he reacted to certain circumstances. But for all he knew, his demeanor would not last, and he would turn. Explode. So he tried to embrace it, to welcome it, to take advantage of it in the best way he could before it was gone.

Jay said something and disappeared, only to return within the same minute. The ceramic amaryllis was in his hands, the swirls so red they could have been repainted overnight. They were magnetic, the swirls, and all Girard could think of was Miriam's ruby lips from the night of the accident—how plump they were, how passionate they tasted, how they rose over his and overpowered them as if they were in control. Girard missed those lips.

"Here she is, Mr. Remington," Jay said, his concentration firm on Girard. "Will you be alright holding her, or should I?"

Girard's eyes were locked on the urn, hypnotized by it and its symbolism. What remained of his wife was inside, and while he knew that was what it meant, he struggled to wrap his mind around the concept. It was finality.

"I think maybe I should." It was Stacey. She reached forward to accept the urn from Jay.

Girard let her without resistance, but also without agreement.

"What do we do now?" Stacey said.

Girard's concentration broke, and he looked up at Jay.

"Well," Jay said, "you celebrate her life, mourn her death, and do the best you can to move on. That's all you can do."

#

There was no service that followed. Like Girard, Miriam did not interact much with other people outside her daily routine. But her reasons were different. After the accident, she became reclusive and self-conscious and emotionally withdrawn. The friends she did have moved on without her, being unable and unwilling to incorporate the constant negativity into their own lives. Antidepressants and psychotherapy got her through for a while, years, and Girard tried to help, and she eventually found the courage within herself to forgive and accept and move on. That was what it took for Miriam to become a living, emotional person again—her own acceptance. It was accepting her situation and figuring out how to adjust rather than feeling sorry for herself or being bitter about what happened to her.

When she had gotten to a place where she was ready to welcome people back into her life again, it was too late. Her closest girlfriends had moved on, their own lives sending them off to explore various parts of the world. There were a few gatherings over a handful of years—a long holiday weekend in a cabin in St. Paul, a weeklong stay at a beach resort in San Mateo, a couple's cruise through the Caribbean—but Miriam neither went nor wanted to. They would not understand or know how to communicate with her anymore, she told Girard, and she would be a burden. After the third rejection, the invitations stopped. Miriam's closest friend's name was Rose, and she was the one who always reached out and invited Miriam to go along. But even Rose stopped writing when it became clear Miriam wanted no part of her old life. So it was just she and Girard for all those years, and Stacey, until it became just the two of them again. And that was how it ended.

Sad as it may be, that was why there was not a service—there was not anybody to go. It was the harsh, bitter reality of the situation.

Nevertheless, it was not as gloomy as it may sound. Miriam was happy. Or as happy as she could have been, with everything that happened. As far as Girard knew, Miriam was as happy on the day she died as the day they first met on the street, although happiness meant something much different to her as she matured.

#

Girard and Stacey stood shoulder to shoulder in front of a sad plot of grass. A paved driveway weaved in and out of the pathways of headstones and monuments that climbed hills and ran parallel to one another. Some of the headstones were decorated with colorful plants and flowers and ribbons, while others were accompanied by short American flags or military wreaths. The oldest ones were faded and unreadable and blanketed with moss and algae. The granite on the newest ones came in various shades of gray and black and red. There were elderly people who lived long, enriched lives, and there were children who were unfairly stripped of their right to make their own journey. There were victims of drug overdoses and incurable diseases and wretched life circumstances who were only set up to fail. There were unlucky ones who were in the wrong place at the wrong time, and those given impossible circumstances. And there were those who took their own lives, cheating away their troubles and sorrows, and those who deserved what they got when they got it. There were all types.

There was a large columbarium in the middle of the cemetery where Miriam could reside but never would. In the far corner was a decrepit mausoleum that looked as if it were built before the first headstone was buried. The rotted exterior was a harbor to termites and black mold and airborne illness, the interior not something Girard would ever willingly explore.

The plot of land at his feet was the one he and Miriam picked out after the death of their unborn baby. Iris, they called her, after her death. Before, they had not decided. And it no longer mattered. Iris was not buried in the plot, just as Miriam would not be, neither Girard. There were four sites in all available for burials within the plot—one each for Miriam and Girard, and one for the two children—and whether Stacey would choose to be part of the family in the afterlife or not, the option would be there, the final decision hers. For now, there would be two headstones for symbolic purposes only, and the cremains would be buried elsewhere.

The amaryllis urn was heavier than Girard remembered. The cremains inside packed double the weight of the ceramic flower, and Girard physically struggled to manage it. But he would hold it until his arms fell off if he had to, even if that meant rotating with Stacey. But that seemed an improbable option at the time, as Stacey was a wreck. Her knees dug into the wet grass, her dress yanked up high enough to let it happen. The mascara that streamed down her cheeks looked like mud, and her bangs swung in front of her face as if they were drying glass.

It was not about her mother, Girard imagined, although she was sad about that too—she had wiped tears from her cheeks every minute since the time they left the funeral home. It got worse, much worse, when Girard showed her the plot. He thought it was the headstone that got her—the tiny, sad headstone with only a date of death and somber quote at the bottom. The quote brought back so many horrible memories that they made Girard physically ill. His stomach cramped with sorrow and agony. The quote, the song, came from a dark place on the darkest of days, but Miriam insisted. It was a sign from God, she said, and she wanted to give baby Iris a chance to blossom in heaven, since that was her only destiny, never having left. Miriam was a firm believer, even after baby Iris's death—especially after. So the quote made it on the headstone, and to Girard, it was a grotesque reminder of that night every time he saw it.

What a shame, what a sight. A good love died tonight.

"I wonder what she would have been like," Stacey said through sniffles.

Not like me, I hope.

"Mom would have loved having a second baby. I'll never forget the way she looked at me when I was a little girl, the way she'd glow when she spoke to me. She'd lean forward so our faces would be close, and she'd put her hands on her knees and we'd rub noses and smile and giggle. Oh, that smile."—Stacey laughed—"Mom was so pretty. Iris would have been too."

Iris.

It was the first time anyone had spoken her name aloud, besides Girard or Miriam. But even that was many, many years ago. Coming from Stacey, it tore deeply at his heart, agonizingly. Having Stacey know about Iris made it all so real.

"That's such a pretty name, Iris. How'd you guys come up with that?"

Stacey seemed to have found some relief by talking about it. The paleness of her skin started to return to its normal yellowish tint. But Girard hated it. He did not want to talk about Iris or Miriam or himself even. He did not want to talk at all. Silence was what he needed right now, so he could try to process his thoughts.

"Did you hear what I said?"

He did, but he did not acknowledge her. His gaze was fixated on the dying grass, his concentration locked in on ensuring he did not drop Miriam. The moment, while he knew it was real, felt anything but. It was over.

"Dad?"

"Not here," he said. "Not now. Later. I'll tell you about it later."

CHAPTER TWENTY

Later came. It always did. Whether Girard wanted it to did not matter. The Saturday flower was in his hand, the stem rolling over the insides of his fingers, the grain from the soil falling to the dining room table. It was a sad flower, as black as midnight and with naturally curled petals that looked as if they were weeping. Fitting, surely, but depressing. Black Saturday was the most difficult day of the week. What began on a Thursday night thirty-seven years ago—the party, the drinking, the accident—ended in misery on a Saturday.

#

While most people were either lounging or taking a romantic stroll or working on a personal endeavor or passion, Girard was somewhere else, pacing a three-foot square next to Miriam's bed as he tried to process what the doctor told him. It was not possible, was it, that the baby was dead, that she would never see the world outside her mother's womb? It did not seem so.

The nurses stopped visiting as frequently as before and the doctor mostly stayed away, and Girard was left to grieve on his own. Miriam was still attached to monitors and a breathing tube and an IV, and there was no end in sight. Her brain had swelled badly, the doctor said, and it would take many days, if not weeks for the swelling to subside. Only then would Miriam have a chance at beginning her recovery. But nothing was guaranteed.

Girard left the hospital sometimes. Stacey needed comforting too and his parents needed relief, and Girard needed to bathe. He would sit by Miriam's bedside while Stacey was in school and would worry about her constantly when at home. He would lay awake at night when Stacey was asleep in the comforts of her bed, unable to shut his brain off long enough to rest. He had never been lonelier. Constant worry nagged. It was the longest, most miserable stretch of his life.

There were decisions to be made—difficult ones, unfair ones, impossible ones to make on his own—but there was no alternative. It was up to him. He did what he thought Miriam would do if the roles were reversed. An induction and traditional birth was not an option, considering Miriam's state, so they had to slice her lower belly and remove the baby manually—that was not a decision; that one was made for him. But what to do afterward was a choice, as was what to tell Miriam when she came to, and what to do until then. It was excruciating.

The hospital had social workers on staff who provided options and asked basic questions that would help lead Girard to the answers he needed, and there was a grief counselor who Girard wept with. It felt wrong, grieving over his and Miriam's loss with another woman, but it was not like that. He needed to be outwardly strong for Stacey, and so the counselor was all the support he had. His parents were already doing enough by helping with Stacey, so he could not burden them further. He had to figure it out on his own.

Girard authorized the baby—who, at the time, was unnamed—to be cremated, and he kept her cremains on Miriam's bedside table. The wooden box was a beautiful cherry red and was the saddest, most heartbreakingly tiny box he had ever seen. Urns should not be made that small, and that was God's fault.

As the days passed, Girard grew angrier and more resentful of Miriam for not being around, and he received additional counseling for dealing with the incredible guilt he felt afterward. The guilt, at the time, was about his feelings toward Miriam, and less so about the choices that led up to her status. Despite having spent days upon days alone, especially emotionally, the crippling guilt he felt about the actual accident and his role in it did not come until later. Specifically, four days later, when two police detectives showed up at Miriam's bedside.

#

"Iris before the storm," Girard said to Stacey. The flower twirled in his hand, looked almost invisible against the backdrop of his blazer.

"What?"

"That's what this is called. Iris before the storm."

"Okay." Stacey's eyes were dry, but her cheeks were red and puffy and huge.

Girard took a deep breath and sighed, felt the weight of a burden release from his body. "You know, people wear black to funerals because it's a sad color. Nobody sees black and gets happy. It's a depressing color."

"Some people like it."

"No, they don't. They may like how they look in it, the way the dark tends to cover up a muffin top or the excess fat they're embarrassed about."

"Dad."

"But no one actually likes the color. How could they? How could anybody? Black represents death and morbidity. Everyone knows that."

"Morbidity? Is that even a word?"

"Just listen," Girard said as he leaned forward. "Black is not happy. Do you think people who are happy wear black all the time? Think again. Happy people wear yellows and blues and reds and greens. Hell, happy people can even wear brown. But black? No, black is not happy. Black is the worst."

Stacey swallowed hard, though Girard did not think twice about it—he saw it, noticed it, but did not think about its meaning at the moment, if there was one.

"Then why do you have a black flower in your hand?" Stacey asked.

"This? This is life. This represents life."

"I thought you said black represents death."

"Don't you see? It does. Black does represent death. It represents darkness and death and suffering. It represents my life. Mine and your mother's . . . you know, before."

Stacey sunk in the chair. Her dress rose and swallowed her as if she were just a child. A sweet, innocent, overwhelmed child.

"That's why we chose Iris for the baby's name. Because of the flower."

Stacey sat reactionless for a few seconds, then sat up straight and leaned forward. "That's horrible. You named my baby sister after death?"

Girard shot up. "It's not horrible! The bearded iris is one of the most elegant, glorious flowers in all of nature. It's about so much more than that!"

"Alright, calm down. Relax."

Girard took another breath, then forced himself to sit back down again. Was he losing it? "Alright, you're right. I just don't think you're getting it."

"Then explain it to me. Make me understand."

"Do you believe in destiny?"

"As in my life's already predetermined for me? As if my decisions have no impact on how I'll end up?"

"Yes. Do you?"

"No. I believe what I do impacts how my life will turn out. The choices I make, the things I do—those are what determine what happens to me. What do you believe?"

"I wish I knew."

"You wish you knew what? If destiny was real?"

"I wish I knew what I believed."

Stacey's mouth opened as if she was going to say something, but then it closed again without anything coming out. What could she say?

"I'd like to believe," Girard said, "but it's hard for me to get there. So many terrible things have happened to me. Your mother believed, though. A strong believer."

"That doesn't surprise me."

"Believing was what got her through, after the accident. It's her faith in God that eventually led her to forgive me. And him."

Stacey looked uncomfortable. She shifted around in her chair as if Girard had struck a chord with her. But Girard understood—forgiveness was an uncomfortable thing.

"What does any of this have to do with the flower? Or the color black? I'll be honest with you, I'm kind of worried about you. I'm a little lost here."

Girard waved her off. "I'm getting there. Just trust me."

Stacey folded her arms.

"As I was saying, your mother was an unquestionable believer of destiny and fate and God—all that stuff. So as tragic as it was—what happened with the accident and with the baby, I mean—she thought there must be a reason. God had chosen her to deal with it. He thought she could handle it—that's what she said. So, the color black, it represents—"

"Death and sadness and, what did you call it, morbidity?"

"Right. But also finality. And fate. If our baby's fate was living a life forever in darkness, then your mother wanted to reward God."

"Reward him?"

"That's the way she saw it. That if she rewarded God with the angel he wanted instead of fighting him or being angry with him or holding it against him, she would be in his good graces too. She thought if she accepted God's choices, if she embraced it, maybe one day they would be reunited and live forever in eternity together—her, Iris, and God."

"I don't even know what to say."

Girard sighed. "That's why we named her Iris. After the most beautiful black flower in existence—the bearded, before the storm iris. We've mourned for Iris every Saturday for thirty-seven years. We gave her to God and we dealt with the storm it brought to our lives, and we mourned for her. Not a day goes by I don't think of her or miss her or wonder what could have been."

Stacey began to cry, her puffy redness lubricated with tears.

"So, we didn't name her after death but instead after the life she was destined to live. In darkness."

Stacey's tears got worse, heavier, formed into sobs. She got to her feet and shook her head, then said, "I can't do this," and left.

And she was gone.

#

Everything Girard said to Stacey was true. The black iris was the most important, symbolic flower in the green house—and the only type of flower in the waterfall garden. Like all of them, and the green house itself, the flowers meant so much more than just flowers. Their colors and their purposes, the specific sequences in which they were clipped during the week—none of it was incidental. It was something Girard spent years fine-tuning, as physiological challenges made some flowers unrealistic to grow in the environment in the green house. It all started with the iris, though, and everything else filled in around it.

The concept of the green house came together a few years after the accident. By then, Miriam was home and as healthy as she would ever be, but she still struggled every day. Coping with the physical change was one thing, but couple that with the emotional scarring she endured from not being there for baby Iris when her life on earth ended, and Miriam was in a dark place. The isolation and depression and lack of sense of purpose took a stranglehold of her life. It was during those years when she ignored the get-together invitations from Rose, and when she became a recluse within her own home.

Girard tried to support her but did not know how, and the more isolated she became, the more resentful Girard became. He had gotten so angry with her for not understanding its impact on everyone else—he with his lack of emotional and physical support; Stacey with her lack of having a dependable mother; Rose and the loss of friendship—that he began to dislike himself. He struggled too, emotionally and as a parent and an educator, but it did not debilitate him like it had Miriam. He experienced moments of sadness and sorrow and guilt and anger too, but he kept it bottled up inside so life could move on. In retrospect, he wondered if that was why he was the way he was today, and if he had done something differently then, maybe he would be better off. But what could he do? He did what he thought was right at the time and did the best he could with it. Whether it was the right thing, who was he to say? He was just a man who tried to do what he could to get through it.

When it got bad—the isolation and the lack of connection and the lack of a sense of togetherness—Girard put his energy into the green house. He was a gardening connoisseur in a way anyhow and routinely kept smaller ones with the tallest, most colorful, healthiest flowers around. The beds around the front walkway were always at their best, and the boxes under the windows were pristine, but he needed something more. Stacey had grown and needed and wanted less attention, and to keep his mind preoccupied and sharp, Girard plotted out his vision for a behemoth garden—what would begin as a traditional greenhouse but morph into something so much more.

The green house.

While it was true Miriam was not herself or present in life's moments, she was not careless or unintelligent either. She resisted hard when Girard first brought the idea to her, saw no reason to spend the kind of money Girard proposed for an asset that would never increase in value. It was true. Undeniable. But that was not what it was about.

The urn with Iris's cremains had yet to have a permanent home. They bounced around between one side table to the next, always visible but never spotlighted quite enough. Girard found Miriam would frequently move the urn—sometimes daily, other times it would be months in between locations—and the situation felt unsettled. For such a major decision, not having the answer to where it should go was bothersome. Agonizing, really. By this time, they had acquired the plot and had Iris's headstone placed, but they agreed her cremains would never go there. The headstone was about tradition, about being there for future generations to commemorate. But that was not where she belonged. She deserved more than being just another deceased person in a field of others. She deserved something special.

Something clicked one day when Girard wandered around the house, looking for his unborn daughter's cremains.

A greenhouse.

What could be a more perfect way to memorialize Iris than by giving her her own garden within the greenhouse, surrounded by black bearded, before the storm irises? Miriam broke down in tears when Girard told her about it, nodded her head ferociously. He sketched pages and pages of ideas, none of them quite right, all of them missing a little something.

Waterfall, Miriam suggested one day, seemingly unexpectedly.

Waterfall?

For the greenhouse. For Iris.

Girard thought about it, did not understand it. Miriam explained her vision to him. If Iris's ashes were going to be buried in the soil, the waterfall would serve the purpose of purifying and renewing her spirit for all of eternity. Waterfalls were rejuvenating and having one running continuously would ensure Iris's spirit would be constantly pure and fresh and cleansed. It was yet another way to ensure God got the angel he was after when he took Iris from them, and it would help them all when it came time for a reunion.

That was how the greenhouse became the green house. And it took on a life of its own from there.

Girard was on board. More than that, he was thrilled. Miriam was energetic about the idea, giddy even, and that was a sign she was starting to come back. Over the next couple of years, Miriam rose then fell, climbed back up only to fall even harder. God made coping difficult for her, which made it difficult for Girard too. By the time the green house was finally complete—the outside structure constructed, the temperature-controlled ventilation and irrigation systems engineered, the variety of flowers planted—Stacey was gone, beginning her life.

It was hard for Stacey, Girard knew, as her adolescent brain could not grasp the bigger concept that consumed most of Girard's waking hours. In retrospect, Girard understood why Stacey was so angry growing up—she must have felt abandoned and forgotten about and ignored. And maybe that was why, he wondered, he felt the need to tell her the accident story in adulthood—maybe it was for his own personal redemption as a man and a father. Maybe he hoped she would understand and forgive him the way Miriam had. It was a lonely thought.

#

As he sat on the stone in front of Miriam's frog garden with her cremains in his lap, Girard was struck by how green the green house looked. It was always green, of course, painted that way not by mistake, but its brightness was particularly vibrant today. Maybe it was the way the sun hit it, or maybe it was the brilliance of the green house itself that bled through the walls and hypnotized everything inside. Or maybe it was a sign sent from the universe that this was where Miriam was supposed to be, joining Iris as part of the natural world.

The green house was a special place. Magical. To say it was supernatural or mystical would not be fair. Girard did not get a sign from God that he should build it, but it was unique. Did spirits who crossed over have influential power from the afterlife? Girard could not help but wonder as he considered all the times he changed course in his thinking. The green house had an aura that had dominion over him, the best part being that he did not mind relinquishing that power—he enjoyed it even, found pleasure in it.

The thing about it was, the green house was more than just a green house—a house painted green—or a house painted green that was also a greenhouse—a green greenhouse, as it were. It was those things, but also more than that. Much more. In the same way the color black was significant, as were the other flowers and their colors, the green house was green for a reason. The concept came together way back when, shortly after the waterfall discussion with Miriam.

Girard understood it and Miriam understood it, but he feared that even if he explained everything to Stacey, she either would not grasp the concept or it would not have the same impact. Why did it worry him? Simple: He did not know how much longer he had left, how many more days he would experience the jubilance he felt when he was inside its walls. What happened when he was gone? Would anyone know the true meaning of the green house and all it stood for? What would happen to Miriam or Iris on the other side? Or less important, what would happen to Girard?

He did not expect to have the same fate as Iris and Miriam—he was not naïve. Between the damage he caused, the lives he ruined, the doubts he had, he was not worthy of another shot. Did he hope for it, if it were true, to be an exception? Of course. But he also understood why he would more likely be rejected at the gate, or if it were less humane than that. That was ultimately the root of it all, was it not? That Girard did not know, that he was not confident in the idea of it, or faithful in the concept. Maybe that was his problem. Would skepticism, could it, be forgiven?

On earth, Girard knew what he had to some extent. Life was full of mysteries—some would never be solved, others would—but at least there was some certainty. In life, Girard had his family, until he did not; he had himself, with whom he hated; and most of all, he had the green house—the spectacular, imaginable green house. The green house encompassed everything about his life on earth—the walls themselves, painted green, the color that represented life itself and its association with nature and natural energies and harmony; the gardens inside represented his wife and his unborn child, and all his emotions and experiences and ugly skeletons that made up his living being; the concept of the green house itself compiled all of Girard's life's loves and passions into one giant, green structure. Everything Girard cared about, living or dead, absolute or imaginative, was a part of the green house in some way. In the literal sense, without the green house, Girard had nothing.

So there he sat in front of Miriam's frog garden as his mind wandered like a firefly in the dark with no end in sight. On the inside, he was frantic—impossibly confused about his next move, terribly afraid at what lay beyond life on earth—but on the outside, he was as calm as could be—his hands as steady as a surgeon's, his concentration laser-focused. The orange bottle was in his pocket again, still full minus the one he popped the day before for routine maintenance. His body would go into shock if he took them all, cardiac arrest likely. He could end it and join Miriam and Iris, and the three of them would be together inside the green house. Forever.

That was the plan. But after Miriam was taken care of. What else did he have to live for? Certainly not himself. Stacey? She was a grown woman, independent. Did she have some issues that would give her trouble? Of course, but who did not? Girard being around would not affect her will or ability to seek out and get help—professional help, not father-daughter, useless advice help. Real help. She would be fine if she wanted to be.

So, it was settled then. He had no reason not to twist the cap off and pour the pills into his mouth and swallow them dry. He could end his misery right now.

But it felt off, wrong in a way. Something was missing. There was a sense of unfinished business somehow. It was logical actually—that feeling. It was spot on.

The green house.

There was still more he must tell Stacey about it. There were secrets within its walls someone else needed to know so when Girard was gone, the green house would be properly cared for. There was no mortgage on the living house anymore, so Stacey should keep the property under all circumstances, and protect it, for as long as feasibly possible—she needed to know these things. Girard must have a conversation with her first to ensure his affairs were in place, then he could do what he had to do. If something happened that threw off the spirits of Iris and Miriam, Girard would have to deal with that for eternity. And if eternity went on for as long as its name suggested, his misery would never end. Then what would be the point of it all if he was still miserable?

There was something else too.

Miriam.

Her final resting place was in her garden, buried alongside the frog. That was not a debate. It was what Miriam wanted all along. That frog, hand-chosen by Miriam as her spirit animal, represented all Miriam hoped for in the afterlife. While she dreamed of becoming a beautiful amaryllis, the green house and its powers would help her get there. And part of that was that the

spirit of the frog would help cleanse her soul and prepare her for renewal
and rebirth, and ultimately metamorphosis into an amaryllis. It was all
mapped out—her soul would join God and Iris in heaven, and her spirit
would transform into her favorite flower—and she would live forever in
harmony.

Girard truly admired her. Her beliefs and hopes and dreams were
complete and precise. Girard's were murky at best. He once heard that
women who knew what they wanted got what it is they were after in life,
and he believed it. Did the same thing apply to the afterlife? Nobody could
say. As mystical as it was to him, as arcane as the entire concept seemed,
Miriam believed it. She believed it would and could happen, and the way she
lived her life, Girard believed it should happen. And she deserved it for all
the cruelty the natural world forced her to suffer through. She earned the
serenity.

That was his motivation—to see Miriam's last wishes through. The best
he could, he needed to put all the pieces in place to give the green house
time to flourish and work its magic, then he could dissolve his existence. He
spent the better part of the last three decades trying to fix all the wrong he
had done to Miriam. He loved her as hard and as passionately as he knew
how, and he put her needs before his own as often as he could. What would
all that mean if he abandoned her when she needed him the most—after
death, when it was in his hands what happened to her? It was his
responsibility as her husband and intimate partner and soulmate to see it
through, to see to it that her last wishes came to fruition. His own doubts
aside, that was what Miriam wanted, so that was what Miriam would get.

Girard needed to prepare the green house.

CHAPTER TWENTY-ONE: Sunday

White was pure. Purity, in its simplest form, was youth. Winter was represented by whiteness—the drifting snow, the iced-over roadways, the blustery winds and frosty treetops. Pure youths and the simplicity of winter were perfectly joined, except when they were not; except when the whiteness cleared the pathway to inevitable gloom. Then, white was worn to grieve over the premature darkness.

Sundays were difficult. For the past thirty-seven years it was that way. In some ways, Sundays were more difficult than Saturdays. The mourning that came along with Sunday was immeasurable. At least on Saturdays there were distractions, a chance to relive the sequence of events over and over. But Sunday was a full day of thinking. Thinking and reminiscing and grieving and sadness. Girard knew today would be hard.

Stacey was gone, a dry spot in the shape of the underside of a car silhouetted on the drive. It was no bother to Girard. The downstairs was quiet and as still as could be, as if the world had stopped. The six on the microwave slowly flipped into a seven as if reluctant to do so. Girard was shoeless, the linoleum underneath cold and clammy.

This was it.

This was his new life. Just him and his living house and his green house. No one would be there to make him coffee or offer him eggs and toast or remind him to take his medication. There would be no one to answer to, no one to enjoy crossword puzzles with, no one to appreciate the quiet alongside. Girard was on his own.

It was remarkably lonely, even more so than he ever imagined. The idea that it would be just he and his thoughts terrified him. While he recognized he trod a thin line, he was unable to control it. He teetered between being emotionally stable and not, and he knew the mostly full bottle on the counter was not a friend, but a foe. The temptation was strong already, the day young. To avoid it, he hurried to the green house, like he always did, barefoot and all.

Despite its powers, it would not be that easy. Not today. Not on a Sunday. But he had to fight it. His demons would not win, not today. Tomorrow, maybe, but not today. There was still so much to do.

He paced. The stones made a track around the flowerbeds in the center of the green house, woven between the door in one corner to Miriam's frog garden in the one furthest from it. Girard walked it. He concentrated on each step as his heel pressed against the cold floor first, then his toes.

Heel, toes, heel, toes.

That was how it started. Once he got the rhythm, he concentrated on his breathing. With the first heel press, he would breathe in sharply through his nose and inhale until his chest was raised. And on each fourth step, he would exhale out his mouth, then he would start the process over again.

Eight paces, turn right. Ten paces, turn right. Eight, right. Ten, right. Without thought, he went around ten times, then fifteen, then twenty-five. Before he knew it, his mind was clear and his eyelids were heavy, and he let them close as he moved.

Eight, ten. Eight, ten.

He felt one with the green house, in total harmony with the brilliant scents of the roses and marigolds and amaryllises and hydrangeas and chrysanthemums. And the lilies. The white lilies. The Sunday lilies. Girard visualized each emotion the flowers represented as he passed them, his vision black, wished the visualization would make it a reality. He coerced his brain to gather in harmony as his heart, to feel the emotions he so desperately imagined.

He imagined not only what it would be like, but remembered what it was once like—he did not always lack the capacity to feel, only after he started taking the medication that tranquilized his emotions. He remembered the way his heart used to flutter with anticipation, or the way it squeezed his wind when he hurt. He remembered how the wet tears tickled as they rolled down his cheeks, and the way they would sometimes escape when he laughed too hard. He remembered feeling sympathy for others and being empathetic, and the occasional bout of jealousy. He remembered how it felt to be resentful. He remembered caring.

As much as he remembered, as real as the memories felt, he could not get there. He could tell himself he felt a certain way, that the confusion he felt was real emotion. When in fact, deep down, he knew the truth. He knew it was just a figment of his imagination, that he told himself he felt a certain way because that was how he was supposed to feel, or how he used to feel. But his feelings were different now. There was nothing there. Emptiness, all the time. It was as if a dark cloud hovered over him constantly, dragged him down, sucked the life out of him. It was an intruder in his mind, a canker inside him. And there was nothing he could do to stop it from attacking.

He had to have been the loneliest person in the world.

And the one person who kept him moving forward, the one who gave him a reason for living, the one who he owed his entire life to, was gone. Dead. Ash.

"What are you doing?"

Girard stopped, his heel-toe rhythm broken, his focused breathing halted. He opened his eyes, felt them burn against the backdrop of the light.

"Where are your shoes?"

Girard blinked, tried to clear out the blur that thwarted him from locating the source of the voice that joined him. As he returned to awareness, he realized his feet were frozen. He felt the calluses on the bottoms of them, the skin on the backside of his heels already hardened.

"What are you doing out here? You look like a crazy person." Stacey was there, visually a wreck. Disheveled.

"Have you been drinking?" Girard said.

"No."

It was a firm, undeniable rebuff. She did not hesitate or flinch. Girard believed her.

"Where are your shoes?"

Girard looked down, surprised to see the tops of his feet, pale and veiny, though he should not have been. "Just walking."

"Without any shoes?"

Girard said nothing.

"Are you going to be alright? Do you want me to stay for a while?"

"You have your job."

She brushed the words away as if they were pests. "Eh. I quit."

Girard just looked at her.

"Okay, I got fired. But fuck them. I was going to quit anyway."

Girard did not ask why—he did not have to. It was obvious, was it not? The next logical question was about the house—how was she paying the mortgage? But Girard did not ask it—the answer seemed predictable. And he lacked the capacity to deal with it, nor did he have the desire.

"Can I get you some shoes? You look ridiculous."

"Don't worry about the shoes. Come sit, I need to tell you some things."

"Sit where?"

Girard looked around. "Stand then."

"Listen, Dad, I don't know if I can handle any more of what you have to tell me. I'm going off the rails a little bit here with what you've told me already."

"I need you to listen. Just listen, okay? Please."

Stacey went toward him, stood close. He could not smell any alcohol on her.

"What it is?" she said.

"There's more to the story I need to tell you."

#

The two police detectives that showed up at Miriam's bedside were there to investigate the accident. That was what they said. Four days after. Girard was taken aback. He found the timing uncomfortable, and he was emotionally rattled. His greatest regret? Answering their questions truthfully. Perhaps he was naïve to think honesty was the best policy, that if he told them exactly what happened, they would go easy on him, that they would be sympathetic. Or maybe naïve was just a nicer way to call him stupid. He was stupid.

He told them everything—about the party and the vodkas and the nip, and about the wintry conditions and the ruby distraction and the crash itself, then the guardian angel that saved them, though he did not use that term. The detectives listened, took notes, and asked many questions. It was not long before Girard caught on to his mistake and realized he should have prepared a story that exaggerated more and was less factual. But he did not condemn himself for long, though, as he had more important things on his mind.

Miriam.

The detectives left. But they came back day after day after day until Miriam awoke, and Girard repeated his sickening, painstaking story each time, forced to relive his nightmare repeatedly. Girard's naivety was still strong, despite what he thought was his acute awareness of it. The detectives were not waiting for Miriam to wake up to corroborate Girard's story and let him off the hook but instead they searched for a lie, for a slip-up. For evidence.

When Miriam did eventually come to, she was not herself. She would not speak and hardly seemed to recognize verbal cues at all. The doctor said it would take some time. Teary-eyed, Girard explained to her what happened with their unborn baby. Miriam did not react emotionally or verbally or otherwise, but she slept with the urn for weeks. For whatever her mental state was, she seemed to understand.

During one of Miriam's daily psychological exams, the detectives came back again. By then, Girard felt more like himself than he had in weeks, his grief having transitioned to caretaker for his unwell wife. And he was on the defensive. He refused to talk to or agree to see the detectives this time, but when they came in anyway, Girard had the sense something was different.

He was arrested on the spot by the two detectives he had become so familiar with. There were times when his naivety got the best of him and he thought they were looking out for him, that they were even becoming friends. But he learned that day, when they twisted his arms so tightly he thought the bones would snap, about life and the people that came and went—everyone had their own agenda and it was every man for himself. There were a select few people that could be trusted in one's life, and even those had to earn it. Girard closed himself off that day, and he was never the same. He recognized it. Skepticism and paranoia crept into his daily life after that, and that was who he became.

Girard was brought downtown and booked, his fingertips inked, his possessions confiscated, his rights explained in vague detail. He was not kept for long, though, as he paid his bail and was released the same day. The charges? Driving under the influence. Girard met with an attorney, reviewed the options. The case was weak—minimal evidence, all circumstantial, no witnesses, no breathalyzer test—but the damage was done, the message sent loud and clear.

Everything was arranged outside the courts. Along with his attorney, Girard sat across from a grumpy man in an expensive suit who represented the state. The state wanted to hold Girard responsible for what happened to Miriam and baby Iris, but there was no medical proof Iris would have survived. Those accusations never left the meeting room, but they were so strong, so personal, Girard never got over it. To avoid a trial and the ugly accusations being brought into the public eye, Girard pleaded to a wet reckless charge. It was less than a DUI and Girard avoided jail time, but the impact lasted a lifetime.

Girard felt guilty. Not in the sense of normal, everyday guilt for doing something he knew was wrong. But instead, he felt guilty for the crime he was accused of. What if they—they being the detectives and the district attorney and the state of Montana—were right? What if Iris died in the womb because of his recklessness? Miriam's doctor said it was medically impossible to say for certain, and the best he could do was speculate, which he would not. At least not overtly. But Girard knew. He sensed the doctor's discomfort when he brought it up, felt the avoidance, writhed at the lack of eye contact. The doctor would not say it, but it was clear what he thought: If Girard had not crashed the car and Miriam had not gone into a coma, the baby would have survived. Girard's recklessness killed his unborn baby.

How could someone move on from something like that? Girard could not, never did. It ate at him every day for thirty-seven years, disturbed his dreams, crucified his psyche. He got away with it in life, but he would never get away with it for eternity, regardless of how much he made up for it. He knew that. People were flawed and could be duped, but not God. God would know the truth. Girard's attorney manipulated the law and exploited the loopholes that were meant to lock up people like Girard—bad people, the worst type of people—and so Girard got a second chance. But what about Iris? She did not even get a first chance. Girard stole that from her. And Miriam? Her life would never be the same, and Girard knew she would blame herself, regardless if Girard tried to take it from her or not. Girard often wondered if he was actually given a second chance, or if he was destined to suffer in the natural life as a consequence of his actions. He was convinced it was the latter, and he had thirty-seven years of evidence to support that.

#

"Your mother," Girard said, "she eventually forgave me. We struggled for years with the resentment, but we found common ground. Life is fragile."

"Why are you telling me this?"

"We're similar, you and me."

"We are nothing alike."

"What you're going through, your addiction—"

"You killed my unborn sister. You . . . you . . ."

You what?

Girard understood why Stacey was upset—it was a lot to handle at once. And he did not take it personally, nor did he care about her judgment. Miriam eventually came to grips with it, so Stacey would too. Although he may not be around to see it.

"You're a killer."

"I wouldn't say that. It was an accident."

"You were drunk!"

"I was not drunk. I was buzzed."

"Same difference! Are you really trying to justify it?"

"Not at all. Don't you see? That's why I'm telling you. To try to make you understand what happened. The guilt I felt, still feel, is indescribable. Really. It can't be put into words how much I've suffered."

"You? How much you've suffered? What about mom? What about Iris?"

Iris.

At the moment, Girard hated the sound of her name spoken aloud. And from Stacey, it made it worse somehow. Stacey did not know the half of it. She had no right to speak of Iris as if she knew her—that was something precious between Girard and Miriam only. Even still, he needed Stacey to know, for her to see it for herself.

"I need to show you something," he said as he stepped toward the waterfall garden.

"Ugh. I can't. I just can't."

"Stacey, it's important."

"Stop, okay? Just stop. Whatever you're doing, I don't want to know. Don't tell me anything else."

"Just listen."

"No. I can't. I can't be here, not with you."

Stacey took off, ran toward the green house door.

"Stacey! Wait!"

But she did not wait. She ran out of the green house and let the door close behind her. As it did, Girard knew he was left without options. Upholding Miriam's final wishes was entirely up to him now. And he had no choice but to see it through to the end, for reliable help was anything but.

CHAPTER TWENTY-TWO

What is the opposite of relief? Burden? Whatever it was, it was heavy on Girard's shoulders, weighed him down like an anchor on his shoulders. The back of his neck strained under its weight, and an achy headache formed underneath where the excess skin wrinkled.

He sighed. There was nothing left inside him to give to the external world, and he was tired of fighting. Even if he wanted to, he could not. Everything about him was exhausted, inside and out. With Miriam gone and his secrets spilled, he was ready to face his inevitable fate, for whatever would be next for him. Stacey was unwilling to accept the responsibility for what remained on the earth for Girard and Miriam and their spirits, so Girard would have to take it upon himself. Like everything else. It was fitting.

His feet were cold, and as he stood, he felt weak. Like his mind, his body was drained. His knees shook, the joints barely hanging on. The bones that had been through so many sleepless nights and tension-filled days were brittle. His body was older than the number on his birth certificate, but he had lived a full life. Long enough? Without question. Satisfying? Hardly. Very soon it would all be over, and none of it would matter. But first, there were final details to button up.

Girard fell to his knees. It was a harder crash than he would have liked, but the pain did not matter. Physical pain would go away, it always did—that was never the problem. It was the scars that could not be seen that hurt the most—those were the ones that never fully healed, the emotional cartilage torn, the recovery time indefinite. The physical pain meant nothing.

The waterfall garden was an arm's length away, but it looked like a mile. The swooshing of the springs over the translucent stones was hypnotic,

Girard's gaze kidnapped. He kept glued to the waterfall as the water level rose then fell, and it seemed to get further away with each passing moment. Making his way toward it seemed implausible. Girard reached for it and an awkward grunt spilled off his tongue and landed sharply against the pits of his ears. The sound surprised him. He reached forward as far as he could until the strain was too much, then he pulled his arm back in tight to his torso, his elbow tucked.

He began to crawl. Palms first, fingertips second. The pressure from his soul was too much and his wrists folded back as if they were made of marshmallow. The tips of his toes dug into the grout as he pushed himself forward, the skin cracking against the tiny raised mounds. The cold floor chilled his bristled nostrils as he breathed.

Onward he went, inching slowly toward the mesmeric waterfall at a snail's pace until he smelled it—the soil, the freshness of it, the bitter dampness of it. Girard laid his cheek against it, listened intently for the naiad that burrowed beneath it. A rush of urgency came over him as if she were speaking to him and caused him to respond with intense concentration.

He had to see her.

Girard began to dig. Using his fingernails as tiny trowels, he buried them beneath the surface and pulled back, over and over and over again. His fingers cramped as he dug, but he would not stop. Could not. He knew precisely where it was buried, him having done so himself, and he knew how far he needed to go. He yanked his knees underneath him and used the remainder of his strength to leverage his hands and fingers into digging. In minutes, the hole was large enough to fit both of his hands inside, side by side. He leaned over the hole, his heart racing, his brow drenched, his palate parched, and looked inside.

There she was.

The wooden edges were faded, once cherry red, now less so, the grind of the earth over the years having damaged the capsule. Girard reached for it, wrapped his dirty fingers around the edges and slid them down until he felt the corners of the bottom. The coarseness felt the same as it did the day he picked it out—one of the lonely days after the accident when Miriam was still unconscious. His shoulders burned as he unearthed the box, yanked it above ground, and placed it at his knees.

Iris.

It was scenarios like these for which Girard usually needed Miriam's guidance. Would removing Iris, even for a brief time, disturb the spiritual rejuvenation at work? He did not know, though Miriam would. He could not imagine a setback taking place now, not after so many years had passed since she was disturbed. Whatever her destiny was, it had to have already been determined, right? Thirty-seven years untouched must have been long enough, at least for a final goodbye.

Girard lifted the box and pressed it against his face. It was so cold. He closed his eyes and kept it pressed to his cheek, willed himself an emotional release. But everything stayed bottled up instead, corkscrewing his insides so badly he wanted to scream. He wished for his misery to be over.

"I'm sorry," he whispered to Iris's cremains through the box, "I'm so sorry."

#

Girard sat with Iris for an hour, silent except for the tranquility of the waterfall. This was it. Peace entered his mind as he rocked with his baby, their final goodbye less sorrowful and more thankful than expected. He was thankful for the moment, for willing himself to take the opportunity to experience it, for his body for holding up long enough to allow it to happen.

When the time came, he knew it. A cleansing rushed through his mind and allowed him to see the future clearly. There was an end in sight. For the first time, it felt real, attainable, like it would happen. That feeling? Relief. Pure, lucid relief. The suffering would be over soon.

Girard placed Iris's urn back into the hole in the garden, his concentration on the task at hand. The box was wooden, but he treated it as if it were made from the finest glass known to man so to ensure nothing bad happened to Iris during the transition. When she was comfortably returned to her final resting spot, Girard packed soil in around her and filled the hole with the mound he created before. He spent the time smoothing the surface until it blended in with the rest of the garden as if it were never unearthed in the first place.

The physical exhaustion remained, but his cerebral stamina was rejuvenated. Girard forced himself to his feet and made his way to Miriam's frog garden, where he began to plot Miriam's finality. It took some shifting to make everything fit. The flowers were rooted deep and would remain intact under all circumstances—there was never any question about that. And while the smiling frog must remain too, the center of the garden was most fitting for Miriam—the flowers of life would surround her.

He kept it plugged in and running, his clothes soaked, while he picked up and moved the frog to the corner. An empty spot was left for future expansion that was large enough to hold the frog, and with expansion no longer needed, Girard put it to good use. Now the center of the garden would be for Miriam, and if what she believed was true came to fruition, someday the most spectacular amaryllis the world had ever seen would sprout.

Girard dug a hole. His fingers were bloodied by the time he finished, and he was so tired he neared collapse. He sat on his backside and rested until he caught his breath, agonized over the thumping pain in the soles of his feet. The garden was prepared and his mind was ready, but his body needed more time. Just a little.

Before heading into the living house, Girard snipped one of the immaculate lilies from the garden and cradled it against his chest. Only then could he make the long, solitary walk to the living house. He needed one more night with his precious Miriam before he would truly be ready to let go. Of everything.

CHAPTER TWENTY-THREE: Monday

Yellow was hope. Hope for a better tomorrow, hope for moving beyond yesterday. It was hope for recovery and for ignoring the temptations. It was unstable in many ways, yet it radiated with energy. With yellow, there was always a chance, and all man needed was the smallest window of opportunity for the chance for a better tomorrow—for hope. It could be a dangerous thing, hope, but when there was nothing else left to live for, that was the one thing that could never be taken away. For one never knew what may lie ahead.

While completely uncharacteristic, it felt appropriate. Girard's final night in the conscious world was spent sleeping restfully with the lily on his chest and Miriam's urn at his bedside. With all the whiteness the lily represented—the grief and the mourning, yes, but more than that, it also served as encouragement for the grieving, and love—and the everlasting love Girard and Miriam shared for each other and baby Iris, it seemed fitting they were all together one final time. And as improbable as it may have seemed, the stem was still moist when Girard awoke.

Nothing changed in the night. The darkness was still present and Girard's focus was as clear as crystal. He awoke with determination to not let anything, or anyone, stop him. Stacey crossed his mind, but only briefly, and though he felt awful that she would likely be the one who would find him, he did not let it bother him, for he knew it was his mind that played tricks on him.

Mondays usually brought with it hope. The weekend sorrow was gone and would be nothing but a distant memory until it came upon again, as it always did, and this Monday was no different. Yet, the hope was different. Instead of hoping to feel better or for finding the aptitude to move on,

Girard felt hope for what was next. Life would be over soon, but what came after was supposed to be the ultimate utopia, and that was something to look forward to. In some ways, he had great anticipation for what the end would bring, with the apex being the chance to see his Miriam again. Even if it was just for a proper goodbye. He felt at peace with where he stood with Iris.

What about Stacey? That question ached inside him, and the what-ifs that came along with it. Would she ever understand? Would she ever get help and be well? Would she ever forgive him? The questions were endless. But she had not been part of his life for a long time, even despite her most recent efforts. It had been less than a full week since they had been reunited, and while he tried, there was a lack of connection between them. It was true she was his only living flesh and blood, but what did that even mean? DNA did not make a connection, at least not in the sense Girard craved as a human being. Love was earned, not given. And Stacey had not done enough to earn hers.

Girard's feet were sore as he descended the stairs and shuffled past the photographs of he and Miriam that hung on the wall. Under one arm was Miriam's amaryllis urn, and the other carried the lily and a mostly full bottle of antidepressant tranquilizers. He rested Miriam and the pills on the kitchen counter while he discarded the bearded iris, cleaned the vase, and swapped out the murky water for fresh. And with a press of his crusty lips against the lily's delicate petals, Girard slid Miriam back under his arm, grabbed the pills, and started for the green house.

There was a sound. So piercingly loud, the whole house shook. But when Girard understood what it was, he realized it was not loud at all. It only seemed that way because of how deathly quiet it was inside the house.

"This is a test," Girard said aloud to no one, his eyes pointed to the ceiling. "I see what you're doing here. You're trying to distract me, to not let me do it." He shook his head. "No, no, no. Not going to work. Not this time."

The sound came again, a chime. Girard smiled, amused at the games the universe played with him. But if the games were real, that meant there was a higher power at work then, did it not? Which also meant . . .

What?

No, no, no.

Girard was not going to fall for it. His mind tried to deceive him. He ignored the noise, tightened his grip on the urn, and stepped toward the back door.

A knock came. From the front.

"Oh, for the love of God," he said. "Nobody's home! Go away!"

Another knock came, followed by another chime.

By now, Girard was disgusted. The knocks and the chimes would not stop unless he addressed it, and he would not be able to concentrate if whoever it was did not go away. He pocketed the bottle and stormed toward the front door.

He whipped the door open as if it were on fire and said, "What!"

Sergeant Bell and the younger Officer Chatham stood on the stoop. Their shoulders touched, their eyebrows raised.

"Everything alright, Mr. Remington?" Sergeant Bell said.

"What do you want? I'm busy."

"What do you have there?" Sergeant Bell motioned to the urn.

"Miriam. My wife."

Officer Chatham's eyes looked sad after Girard said that, but not Sergeant Bell's. The sergeant was bothered by something.

"What are you doing with it?" Sergeant Bell asked.

"Grieving," Girard said.

Sergeant Bell nodded. "May we come in?"

"Listen, guys, I'm really not up to it. My wife has just—"

"I'm not asking. We need to come in."

Girard was taken aback. "Excuse me?"

"Please step aside."

Girard backed away and the two policemen pushed inside.

"We're going to look around," Sergeant Bell said. "If you do not mind."

"For what?"

Sergeant Bell looked into Girard's eyes, hard, and kept them there. "For anything that helps."

Girard was confused.

What is going on?

The officers wasted no time. The younger one stomped through the upstairs, then retreated and made his way into the garage. Sergeant Bell perused each room on the bottom floor. Girard stayed with him.

"Whatever you're looking for, you're not going to find it," Girard said. "I've done nothing wrong."

Sergeant Bell stopped what he was doing, turned, and walked toward Girard. "Who said anything about doing anything wrong?"

"I'm just saying, whatever you're looking for, you're not going to find it."

"What's going on?" Stacey popped in, a powdery donut hole in her hand.

"What did you do?" Girard said, glaring at her.

"Nothing! What did you do?"

"Nothing."

There was chaos. Officer Chatham entered the room with something in his hand, and he and Sergeant Bell chatted about it. Stacey spewed hatred at Girard, none of which he heard or understood. His skin was hot.

"Everybody stop," he said. But nobody did. Then he repeated it, louder, without luck. So he tried: "Everybody shut the hell up!"

That worked. All eyes turned toward him.

"Mr. Remington—"

"Shut up, Sergeant." It was bold. But he did. "Somebody better tell me what the hell is going on here. Right now."

Officer Chatham stepped forward, a yellow-handled metal object in his hands. "Mind telling me what these are for?"

Girard studied them. "Bolt cutters? What are bolt cutters for?"

"Why do you have them?"

"To cut bolts."

"Cut the bullshit, Girard," Sergeant Bell said. "Answer the question."

Girard looked around. The two men were skeptical, his daughter fiery. He still had not a clue what was going on. "Just a tool I've had in the garage for years. Not that uncommon."

"Could they be used to cut brake lines? I think they could."

"I'm no car expert, far from it, but yes, I think they could. Why?"

"Did you puncture the brake lines of your wife's vehicle, Mr. Remington?"

Girard's stomach flipped. "What? Of course not."

"Yeah, well, we'll see about that."

"What's going on?"

"The vehicular report came back from the lab," Sergeant Bell said. "And the brake lines were punctured, which is the probable cause of the crash that killed your wife. Did you kill your wife?"

Stacey gasped.

"Of course not," Girard said. "How could you even think that?"

"Why was she on Highway 15? For a woman who didn't drive, that's an awfully long way from home."

"Dad?"

"Where were you really that day, Girard?" Sergeant Bell's eyes pierced him with accusation.

The betrayal hit the hardest right in the center of Girard's chest. "You think I . . . Why would I?" The weight of Miriam was suddenly overwhelming under his arm, and he struggled to hold her.

"Were you getting tired of her? Was her handicap such an issue for you that the only way to eliminate it from your life was to take hers? Is that what happened?"

"No! Of course not. I love Miriam."

"But love wasn't enough, was it? You couldn't stand it anymore."

"Guys, what you're insinuating, it's crazy."

"We know about the accident in the 80s, Girard. And we know about what happened to Miriam and to your unborn baby. Iris, was it?"

The rage came. And fast.

"Did Miriam want to tell your story? Or was she going to leave you finally, after all these years? I bet she couldn't stand to look at you anymore after all you've done to her. Am I getting warm?"

"Get out," Girard said. "Get out of my house right now."

Sergeant Bell smirked. He thought he was onto something, something big—his face said as much. "Come on, Chatham."

"We're taking this for evidence," Officer Chatham said as he raised the bolt cutters.

"We'll show ourselves out."

CHAPTER TWENTY-FOUR

Girard needed to sit. His arms wobbled as he struggled to carry Miriam to the living room. But they made it, both of them, and he plopped into the chair.

What was that?

He did not have time to process the answer to that question, though, because Stacey barged in.

"What the hell is going on here?" she said.

Girard had never seen her complexion so pale, even as an unwell girl. "Stacey . . . I—"

"Please. Don't lie."

"I've never lied to you."

Stacey laughed. "You've been lying to me all your life. The accident, Iris, Mom. My whole life's been a lie."

"That's different."

"You can't be serious. How is that different?"

"I was protecting you."

"Oh, please! Protecting me from what?"

"From yourself."

Stacey stopped. She stepped back and swallowed, repositioned her weight.

"I've been trying to tell you this. You and I are the same. I've made so many mistakes in my life, so many bad choices. I don't want you to make the same mistakes I have."

Stacey sighed. She sat down across from Girard. The sofa deflated. "Mom didn't really go deaf because of meningitis, did she?"

Girard bit the inside of his lip. "Yes, she did."

"But she didn't get it from E. coli from bad seafood though, did she?"

"No."

Stacey looked away. The disappointment on her face was heartbreaking, and Girard hated she had to find out this way. But she was just a kid when it happened—what else was Girard supposed to have told her?

"How then?"

Girard took a deep breath. "After the accident, when your mother was in a coma, they had to do brain surgery. There was so much pressure in her brain from all the swelling from the impact. That was why she was in a coma in the first place. They had to drill holes in her scalp to help release some of the pressure, to keep her from dying.

"It worked—that's what made it so hard. The surgery worked. Within two days she was awake. But after—two or two and a half weeks I think it was—she started getting sick. Real sick. Bad fever. Vomiting. Seizures. It was bad. Really, really bad. I thought it was the grief, you know? Heartbreak is real.

"Thank God for her doctors. They watched over her constantly and made an early diagnosis. They saved her life. Again. But meningitis, back in the 80s especially, it was horrible. Just horrible. It infected her brain and spread to the nerves and the temporal lobes and all that, and it destroyed her hearing. But she was alive."

Stacey's eyes were filled with tears while she shook her head. Girard felt like a monster.

"And that was that. Permanent hearing loss in both ears. Our lives were never the same."

"Is what the detective said true?"

"Sergeant."

"Seriously, what the fuck ever."

"I didn't do anything to the brake lines. Nor was I tired of her in any way. We took care of each other. We loved each other."

"Why was she on Highway 15?"

Girard shook his head. "I don't know. I don't know why."

Stacey looked at the floor. Girard wanted to see her face, to read her, but the angle was impossible. What was she thinking about?

She looked back up. "Did you kill her?"

"Of course I didn't. Why would you even think that?"

Stacey did not answer. She would not look him in the eye. "I don't believe you," she said. Then she left.

#

What the hell was happening? That was where Girard's mind was at. What could he do? Nobody believed him, yet it was so unfathomable he would kill Miriam he was unable to process it. He had nothing to hide.

Outside, he heard Stacey roar out of the driveway. Rubber squealed. She ran away a lot, he noticed. He recognized the pattern. Instead of addressing a situation and resolving it, she hid. Hid her thoughts and emotions and opinions, and the resentment surely built up like a volcano, bound to erupt at any time. Girard knew the signs—he was like that too. He wondered if that was why her marriage failed, aside from the addiction that wore out her husband. It was yet another indication of how wonderful Miriam was, who tolerated Girard and his own flaws for so long. The bond the two of them had was special. Once in a lifetime.

What now? Was it time to execute the day's agenda? It felt wrong now with this uncertainty looming over him. Though the uncertainty was not from him, but from others—he knew he had nothing to do with it. But how would it look? Would he be labeled forever as a man who killed his wife? Did it even matter? He knew the truth, and if God existed, he would know too. That was all that mattered. Let the world judge.

The green house awaited.

The pills rattled as Girard walked, his pocket stuffed. Miriam weighed heavy under his arm. The green house door opened then closed behind him, and Girard felt at ease. His decision was made, and regardless of the forces that worked together to try to stop him, today would happen. The torture must end.

He went to Miriam's frog garden. The chrysanthemums were brighter than the others. There was something about the chrysanthemum that always gave Girard hope. Whether it was the multilayered petals that formed a staircase to the head, or the brightness of the yellow that could cheer up any mood, it was something. It had remarkable powers. The best part about it was how it made Girard feel—most weeks it was hope, but this time, it was something different than that. Something more. Something more powerful.

Hope could be dangerous. It offered up unrealistic expectations that exposed someone to experiencing a massive letdown, which ultimately was worse than the hope was in the first place. Did it help, to have hope? Sometimes. And there was nothing wrong with it. But when someone went through life using hope as their crutch, whether it was justified or realistic, they were bound to be disillusioned and unhappy and emotionally unwell. Sometimes expectations for life had to be tempered.

The chrysanthemums were not like that, not today. Girard admired them and felt as though they had the capability to work miracles. Like the guardian angel way back when, or the calling to design and build the green house, there was something special about the chrysanthemums. There was one particularly that rose taller than the others and had a thicker stem and stronger petals, and it solidified itself as superior to all the others. Girard bent down, grabbed the clippers, and snipped it.

The hole he dug for Miriam the day before was good—plenty wide and deep enough. His hands clamped around the urn. His shoulders trembled as he held the urn suspended over the hole. This was it, was it not? Once Miriam was in that hole and covered with dirt, she was gone. Officially gone. Forever. It was finality. Miriam was gone and would soon be joined by Girard, so it was time she got her chance to begin the metamorphosis she wanted so badly. Especially before it was too late.

As hard as it was, Girard let her go. In every sense, Girard wanted to fight it. He tried to even—his body shook, his mind failed to process it, his heart ached. But he did it. With the bottom of the vase pressed against the earth, Girard spread apart his fingers and pulled away, and the tips grazed the smooth ceramic swirls on the side on the way out. His chest screamed with agony and his midsection convulsed. Girard fell to the side. His backside slammed hard against the stone, and air plunged out of him. With his face in his hands, he shook.

"I can't take this anymore!" he cried out. The echo of his voice pounded against him from every angle. "Why me?"

He did not expect an answer back, nor did he get one. He was not even sure he had spoken to anyone specifically, for he knew the universe did not speak back. But the anguish strangled him from the inside out, and the pain was so awful he would not wish it upon his worst enemy. He had to get out. He needed to be released from his body.

Before he buried Miriam, Girard tossed the chrysanthemum in the hole. It landed stem down, its wondrous yellow pointed toward the sky. Girard acknowledged the moment and wondered if this was the right thing. The chrysanthemum was not part of Miriam's plan. But since it would be the last flower Girard would ever snip, and since the chrysanthemum was the most magnificent one Girard had ever seen, he thought it would be right. And if this chrysanthemum could produce miracles, he thought Miriam could use the help. She would surely need it.

A jolt of adrenaline shot through Girard at the perfect time. He doubted himself, torn between leaning in and grabbing the chrysanthemum or leaving it, when his body made the decision for him. Without further thought, he surrounded the mound of soil and shoveled it into the hole. Tiny pebbles pinged against the urn, ricocheted like bullets on a battlefield. Girard's hands burned as they did the day before, and the tiny scabs exploded. He picked up his pace. Before long, the mound was flat and level with the surface, and Miriam was gone, buried underneath the green house.

Girard breathed heavily, uncontrollably, and he sat back and tried to catch his wind. His heart raced, and his chest erupted with pain each time it hopped. He eventually settled and returned to his normal.

Then it was his turn.

When the moment came, it was easier than Girard expected. The demons in his brain were silent and the forces that surrounded him had given up trying to stop him. Somehow, though hard to believe, he had won. He had just enough strength to find the courage to put a stop to the pain, and Miriam's final needs were handled. For the first time in a long time, he could worry about himself now, and he could do what he wanted to do.

And that was to end the suffering.

The two longest fingers on his right hand pinched the bottle and pulled it from his hip pocket, trembled only slightly. He was not nervous, that much he knew. Exhausted? Yes. Overwhelmed with grief over Miriam and relief for himself? Absolutely. Ready to stop the pain? Unquestionably.

The cap popped off when Girard applied pressure with his palm and twisted. It fell to the ground and spun on the stone until it stopped. Girard fingered the pills, counted out at least three weeks' worth, which would be plenty. He tossed one in his mouth and swallowed. Then another. But by the time the third one was on his tongue and sat there, he lacked the saliva to push it down his throat.

But he kept trying. His tongue massaged the inside of his cheek, then his gums and the roof of his mouth. A dab more saliva was produced in the process, but not enough to sufficiently coat his throat. With all the perspiration he had sweated while he buried Miriam, he was dehydrated. And as much as he wanted to fight against it, he would be unable to take every pill without help. He needed water.

Using the stone as leverage, Girard forced himself up. Except it did not work. His legs were weak, unable to straighten and hold his weight. It made sense when he considered it. He was an old man, and with the level of physical exhaustion he had just been through, along with the emotional strain, he needed a break. He would close his eyes and allow himself to be serenaded by the waterfall, and he would try to relax. And by the time he was rejuvenated enough to make it to the living house and back, he could finish the job before it was too late. He would not allow himself to be held back any longer.

CHAPTER TWENTY-FIVE

When he awoke, everything was black, and he wondered if this was hell. It smelled different than the natural earth did—it was dank and stuffy, and his breathing labored. A tickle in the back of his throat made him want to cough, but nothing came of it when he tried.

Suffocation.

In a panic, Girard flailed his arms, felt for anything that may help rescue him from wherever he was. Something firm was at chest level, so he planted his palms and pushed with everything he had. How easy it was surprised him, and the next thing he knew, he was flat on his back, eyes squinted, open sky above. Girard wiped something from his face and spat more of it to the side, then he pressed a hand to his chest and gasped for air.

When he came to, he was back in the green house, the elegance of the roaring waterfall unmistakable, the glass above his head so clear it could have been a mirror. His face hurt as if there was some trauma, though his hands were not bloodied when he checked. Everything was a haze.

What was happening?

Girard's recollection of the recent events slowly came back—first the hole, then Miriam being buried inside it, and the pills. Was it the pills? Were they screwing with his mind? No way, not after taking just two. What then? It could be exhaustion. The physical, the emotional—all of it. Maybe it knocked him out.

He sat up, looked around. Everything seemed normal, like he remembered. His shirt was soaked. The center of Miriam's frog garden sat taller than the rest, the smoothing of the soil above her urn sloppy. Girard would fix it. Water shot from the frog's mouth in an arc, the momentum kept it ongoing. The waterfall lingered in the far corner, purifying Iris's spirit as it did. Blossoming flowers were everywhere. And on the stone sat the pill bottle, tipped on its side, a handful of oval pills scattered about. It was as if nothing happened.

And nothing did. Or so it seemed that way. Girard was still parched, even his tongue dry now, like cotton. He scooped up the pills and tried to get up and was able, though slowly. He concentrated on putting one foot in front of the other as he lumbered toward the living house.

Inside, the faucet ran cold as he guzzled glass after glass, and his body felt reenergized a little more with each gulp. He kept at it until his stomach was full and his abdomen felt bloated. A roaring belch flew from his mouth. When the glass was filled to the brim for the last time, Girard pushed the faucet's handle down. Tiny droplets splashed against the stainless sink.

Stacey crashed in. "There you are. I've been looking for you." She stumbled toward the counter, nearly tripped over her feet, and tried to jump up. But her hands slipped and she almost fell, so she stood instead.

"Alright, that's not true. I haven't been. But here you are now!"

Girard clenched his jaw. He knew.

"What's on your face?" she said. She leaned toward him with her arm extended, two fingers pinched close. "And why are you wet?"

Girard backed away. He smelled it on her.

"Is that dirt?"

It was, from the garden, but it did not matter. What mattered was that smell.

"I've been thinking about what you said," she said, "and I think maybe you're right. Yeah, you're definitely right. We are alike. We're both twisted boozers who can't help ourselves but ruin other people's lives."—she smiled, but it was sad, embarrassed even—"Cheers to that, right?"

"I thought you were on the mend?"

"Mend? Ha! I never said that. Far from it."

Girard thought he remembered otherwise but acknowledged it could have just been wishful thinking.

"If we're the same, that means it's your fault I'm like this. I was born this way. Bound to fail. Thanks, Dad."

Girard did not know what to say. Maybe she was right.

"If it wasn't for you, none of this would have ever happened. Mom would be alive. Iris would be here. And me . . . I might actually be normal."

Normal? What did normal even mean? Was anyone normal?

"Maybe Tom would still love me. Maybe I wouldn't have lost the baby and Tom would still want to be with me."—angry tears welled in Stacey's eyes, and her complexion reddened—"You've fucked me up."

Girard felt sad. Though not in the sense of being sad because of grief or loss—he could not remember what that felt like, or maybe he could; he was lost. It was sadness in the sense of feeling pity for someone for being so obtuse or naïve to understand what was happening. That was Stacey. Whether it was the vodka that slurred her brain or the underdeveloped mind that never grew up, she was so far gone it was unfathomable. There was no realistic way she put those pieces together and thought they were connected—no way. Girard did not have the energy to offer up a rebuttal. Stacey would think what she would think, and Girard could not change that. Not at this point. He had already tried.

"You're a piece of shit, you know that?"—water poured down Stacey's cheeks—"How could you?"

"How could I what?"

"Do everything! Live with yourself after what you did to Iris? And Mom. How can you stand looking at yourself in the mirror every day?"

She had not been in the bathroom, clearly. He had not looked at himself in the mirror in years, and excusing the unintentional times when he saw his reflection in a storefront window, or when he slid too far upward in the front seat of the Buick, or when he shaved—he was always careful not to look at himself in the eye. He hated himself.

Maybe Stacey did understand. She projected her anger on him, and that was fair. But maybe deep inside her consciousness she knew what he faced every day, and intellectually could not understand how he did it. She was given a lot of information over the past few days, and maybe this was her mind's way of processing it. Maybe Girard did not listen to the words she spoke well enough.

"God, you're just such a . . . bad person."

Girard's head fell. Of all the names she could call him, that was one that was spot-on. He was. For all he had done, he was a bad person. Even Stacey, who hardly knew him, saw that.

"Mom should have left you a long time ago. Like the detective said, it totally made sense. She must have finally realized how awful you are and figured she could do better."

"That's enough!" Girard said. Rage suddenly poured out of him. "You can put me down and judge my character and criticize my parenting skills—fine! I've done it all too. But you cannot, will not, ever question my loyalty to your mother. I loved your mother with every ounce I had. I gave her everything I had to give. I loved your mother more than I loved myself."

Stacey stepped back, used the counter as a crutch. The whites in her eyes were snaked with red, and her cheeks glistened.

"If nothing else in this world, I was a good husband. Miriam meant everything to me." Girard felt the urge to sit, suddenly exhausted. He scrambled to the living room before he collapsed to the floor.

His chest felt heavy and his heart raced. It was the preliminary stages. He closed his eyes and inhaled deeply, held the breath for a count before he released and repeated. The tricks from Doctor Brown ran through his mind, each of them he tried.

It lasted for two minutes. By the time he counted the second forties, his chest felt lighter and his breathing steadied. But everything trembled, his vision spun, and he knew he needed some air.

Each step hurt. His feet felt as if they were cemented in stone, the effort required to make it to the front door unimaginable. By the time he did, sweat poured from his scalp and dripped down his forehead as if he had just finished showering. The hair above his eyes caught it, soaked it up like a sponge, and wrung it out through his line of sight. He reached for the door handle, felt around where he thought it should be, the blur in his eyes offering no help. He squeezed when he found it, yanked it toward him, and pulled with it the cleansing air that was outside.

He made it off the entryway and down the walkway only to fall to his knees when he stepped on the grass. The blades were sharp under his skin, the pointiest ones sliced through the tiny holes in his pants he did not know existed. He leaned forward and keeled over, gave in to the pressure his body forced upon him.

A shadow moved past overhead, the grass in front of him darkened as it did. A small critter ruffled in the trees not far from where he lay. There was nothing spectacular about the moment that helped him feel better, but it happened. He relinquished his body to the attack that tried to take him, and by not fighting, it passed. The tension in his neck and jaw lingered, but as he breathed in and breathed out and took in the grassy scents of the earth, the knot in his chest dissipated.

He sat up. The sponges above his eyes dripped, so Girard lifted an arm and wiped the water away. His vision cleared and his breathing slowed, and he whispered his silent thanks to Doctor Brown. A bug flew by. It stopped in front of his face as if debating whether to land on his nose, then thought better of it and buzzed past. Even the bugs did not want to touch his face, and he could not blame them.

The irony of the situation was apparent. Of all the panic attacks Girard had throughout the years, he had not once been able to control it without help. Not ever. And now, with this likely being the last one he would ever have, it made it one obstacle he never thought he would conquer. In some ways it was gratifying, though it was not a goal of his. Did it mean something? Who knew? But it gave him a glimpse of hope for whatever was next—maybe he was strong enough to tackle whatever would come on the other side.

Girard stood, prepared to head for the green house. Something about Stacey's car caught his attention as he turned. It was not in the drive as expected but instead was parked cockeyed on the grass at an improbable angle.

No.

No!

Girard balled his fingers into fists and rushed inside the living house. "Stacey!" he called as his legs churned with newfangled purpose.

He found her in the kitchen where he left her, only now she sat on the floor with her back pressed against the cabinets, and her head bobbed.

"You!" Girard said, a finger pointed at her. The muscles in his hands clenched, and he squeezed until the veins rose up from underneath his skin. The tension returned to his face and neck vigorously.

Stacey looked up, her eyelids droopy. "Huh?"

"Get up."

She tried but it was slow. Too slow. Girard stepped closer and reached toward her, slid his fingers under her arm and yanked.

Stacey swatted him away. "Okay, okay. I'm getting up."

Which she did, eventually.

Girard seethed. "After everything I've told you, how could you?"

"Listen, I don't know what you're talking about, but I've got this blistering headache."

"Did you drive like this?"

Stacey looked at him, but her gaze fell off and she shrugged. "It wasn't far."

"After everything! Did you not listen to a word I said to you?"

"It was a mistake."

"Mistake? A mistake is leaving the outside light on or forgetting to lock the door or leaving your purse on the counter. Those are mistakes. Making the choice to drive a car in the state you're in, that's criminal. It's stupid and selfish. And after everything—"

"I'm sorry, alright? Nothing happened."

"And you think that makes it okay?"

"No, I didn't say—"

"Get out. Get your stuff and get out."

"But I can't—"

"Figure it out. I'm going for a walk. When I get back, you better be gone."

Stacey's keys were on the counter. He reached forward and grabbed them.

"Hey! Give me those."

"Call a cab."

CHAPTER TWENTY-SIX

Deep breaths. Deep breaths. That was what Girard told himself. Deep breaths.

Phew.

Why was it so difficult?

The more he knew what he wanted, the more outside resistance tried to interfere. Did that mean something? Was it a sign from the beyond that he was meant to wait? Or worse, not do it at all? Certain things were out of his control, and that was fine. He accepted that. But those he could—deciding when he had lived long enough, for one, or stopping Stacey's drunkenness from destroying her life or the lives of others—were privileges he would not sacrifice, regardless of the challengers that opposed him.

The more he thought about it, the more he was convinced it was the right thing to do. Miriam was buried and the chrysanthemum was picked, sprouting hope for eternity. And while it was true Stacey had proven to be untrustworthy when it came to being the keeper of the gardens and maintaining the green house, Girard felt comfort in the effort he put into it. He tried to make Stacey understand, but she just could not. And he understood it and ultimately would not hold it against her. It was a lot to take on. Maybe it was unfair of him to ask. But there was no one else, so what was he to do? Maybe she would change her mind one day.

Girard came upon a trail that extended from the sidewalk to deep inside the forest. A heavy steel gate blocked the entrance. Hung from it was a faded yellow sign that prohibited unleashed pets to enter. Girard and Miriam had walked the trail together, hand in hand, on few occasions over the years, though Miriam preferred the indoors. Up until the accident, it was not like that. She was not like that. She was energetic and enthusiastic and a lover of nature. But after she lost her hearing, a stroll through the forest stripped her of the joy, she said. Missing out on the crackling leaves and snapping twigs and shuffling bushes that surrounded the path, the experience was no longer the same. This was the first time Girard had been on the path without Miriam, and he thought about her with every step he took.

#

Adjusting to life with Miriam no longer being able to hear was an incredible challenge. Together, they had to learn how to communicate as if they were children. And Stacey, she was impressionable. Confused and impressionable, and she struggled to cope. They all did.

Girard had to adjust to some changes too, but his neither mattered nor were as severe as Miriam's. After all, he deserved them. The scars on his chin and left cheek and above his upper lip would never fully heal, and the hair never regrew. His mustache had a permanent gap missing from it, but he thought what hair there was hid some of the trauma. Though when he caught an unfortunate glimpse of himself by mistake, he wondered if the mustache made it worse, if it drew attention to it.

The scars were the first things people saw when he entered a room, even before Girard himself. They defined him. People associated them with him, were unable to recognize him in photographs from earlier in his life before the scars were there. Those types of judgments no longer bothered him, though they were still there. He recognized the way a cashier at the supermarket would avoid eye contact, or the way the technician at the pharmacy would stare, or the way children would whisper to their brothers and sisters about the monster; then they would point at him and sometimes laugh, and their parents would look mortified and hurry them off without the thought of an apology. That was just how it was, and Girard accepted it. The judgments had not bothered him for a long time. Ultimately, he agreed with them.

Life was hard. Like Miriam, the most difficult permanent damage to live with was unseen. But unlike Miriam, the real trauma took years to develop, like a slow, agonizing death. The impact of the crash was explosive. And without the cushion of the airbag to reduce the impact of the blow, the situation ended up worse than it already was. The left side of Girard's face took the brunt of the force, and when his neck whiplashed to the side and struck the window, his tear duct ruptured.

Girard did not realize it for a while, not until Miriam was back home and they were adjusting to their new lives. At first, his eye would leak more than usual, then it swelled up and eventually crusted with pus. By the time Girard had gotten around to have it looked at, it was too late, and the duct never returned to full function.

There were experimental procedures that could have been performed to repair the duct, but Girard could not get himself to leave Miriam alone long enough. Plus, it did not matter. He was unable to cry out of one eye, so what? His right eye was fine. He just did not realize how deeply of a human need it was, or how disconnected he would feel from his own emotions without it.

It was not the same. His left eye was constantly irritated and dry, and the partial emotional release lacked fulfillment. Once he began taking the medication to treat his depression, the tears dried up entirely. Part of it was psychological—that was what Doctor Brown said. And combined with the general numbness he felt and the physical limitations he had, it was something he could not get past. All the physical and emotional and psychological trauma was too much, and he resided himself to the idea he would never be able to cry again.

#

Girard stopped and blinked, cleared his vision. Where was he? He looked around and saw trees as high as the clouds and a rainbow of colors. Shrubbery surrounded him like a cocoon. Stillness filled the air. His shirt was still damp.

Girard was winded, worked up still, tense in his rib cage. He did not like being there, especially by himself. Time was lost on him, and he was unsure how long he had been gone. Had he given Stacey enough time to get out? There was an intense longing he felt for the green house, and he knew he had to go back. He craved its attention and its presence and its comfort, and he knew that was where he belonged. Whether Stacey was still inside the living house or not was irrelevant—Girard needed to be confined within the four walls that served as a sanctuary for his life. And it had to happen now.

Girard quickly spun, nearly lost his balance. The heavy gate was only an arm's reach away, which both surprised and confused him. He had only made it feet into the forest, yet he was lost within his mind so deeply he had no recollection of it. The thought made him uncomfortable, left him wondering what else he had missed. He was worried he was losing it. He had to go back.

His heels dragged as he started back toward the mouth of the trail, the pavement on the other side scattered with pine needles. It was warmer on the sidewalk without the canopy of the forest overhead, and he felt a drop of moisture on his brow. He picked up speed as he hiked back toward the house. His legs churned with an urgency that came from within. Returning to the green house felt critically important, and he sensed time was limited.

The living house was in view on the horizon, the tail end of Stacey's car partially visible through the hedges. Her keys jangled in his hip pocket as his legs pushed on. Across the road, he heard his name. Or at least he thought he did, but that was not possible. Who would be calling him? He kept moving, afraid it would be too late if he did not get inside the green house soon.

"Girard!"

His name was clearer now, definitely not a figment. But he kept on, did not allow for the distraction. He breathed heavily now, his aging insides not accustomed to this level of physical activity. But he had to fight on. There was no choice.

"Girard! Hold up for a second!"

Girard thought he recognized the voice. It rang out again, and it left no doubt. It was Bernard, the neighbor, the one man Girard ever chose to associate with in his daily life outside of Miriam, although the frequency was hardly ever.

"Girard, hold on over there!"

Against every instinct in his body, Girard pulled up and waited for Bernard on the sidewalk, though he did not know why. His lungs screamed.

"Hi there," Bernard said, out of breath. He held up one finger and leaned over, sucked air in from the ground up.

"I'm in a hurry. What is it?"

Bernard looked up, and the curls in his beard bounced. "I just wanted . . . Just give me a second." Bernard took a minute to catch his wind.

Girard was impatient. He glanced toward his driveway while his insides jittered. It felt as if something was about to slip away—an opportunity or a moment of reckoning or something equally as significant.

"I just wanted to say I'm sorry," Bernard said. "I heard what happened. It was on the news."

That was right, the news. The interview at the scene of the accident. "Thank you."

"If there's anything Jane and I can do, if you need a ride or something."

"Oh, no, thank you. I had a small service for Miriam on Saturday. Nothing much, but that's what she wanted."

Bernard's expression changed. He stood back a step and his face turned. His eyes squinted. His lips puckered. His forehead wrinkled. "I'm so sorry. I thought . . . The news said."

Girard was confused. His recollection of the reporter on the scene was clear. "I'm not following. You saw the report on Wednesday night? It was—"

"Wednesday? I didn't see anything on Wednesday. I'm talking about Friday. It was the lead story all day."

"What are you talking about? What story?"

Bernard looked uneasy now, as if he had been exposed. "Oh, God. Girard, listen, I . . . There's been police at your house off and on the last few days . . . And so I just assumed . . . I would have—"

"What are you talking about?"

"The story on the news, on Friday. It was about Miriam."

Girard's insides stiffened. The pain in his stomach was like being knifed, and it forced him to keel over in agony and cry out.

"Are you okay?" Bernard said. He leaned down and placed a hand on Girard's shoulder.

"Tell me what you saw. I need to know what you saw."

"You have to believe me, Girard. If I would have known you didn't know—"

"Please! Bernard, please."

"Miriam's in the hospital. She's battered and bruised, but okay. At least that's what the news said. They've been trying to contact you, but the phone's disconnected."

Girard trembled. He was completely shaken, unable to speak.

What?

He managed to stand up straight despite his core burning with resistance. He raised his arm and dropped a hand on Bernard's shoulder.

"I have to go," he said. "I . . . I have to go."

Bernard nodded. His brown skin turned almost as light as Girard's.

Girard sprinted off.

Oh my God.

Oh my God!

"Stacey!" he yelled as he crossed into his property, the front door closer with each step. "Stacey!"

In one fluid motion, he reached for the door handle, twisted it, threw it open, and rushed inside.

"Stacey! Plug the phone back in! Do it now!"

CHAPTER TWENTY-SEVEN

It was absolute chaos. Madness. In her state of inebriation, Stacey was slow to process information as Girard hollered at her. The more commands given, the slower she moved.

"The phone," he said as he tried to calm himself. "Can it be fixed?"

Stacey was glazed over, her eyelids puffy, the eyes underneath barely visible. She slowly nodded, the processing time delayed. "Yes. I mean, maybe. I think so. Why?"

"Good. Work on that."

Girard ran to the living room. His muscles ached and his breathing labored, but both were only footnotes. His consciousness was on high alert, his complete awareness of the situation the only thing that mattered. There had to be a misunderstanding.

Girard dropped to his knees and reached around the backside of the television, felt for the loose cords he yanked out days before. His shoulder stretched liked putty and his entire upper body conformed around the stand as if he were made from elastic. He fingered the web of cables, found the metallic prongs, and jammed them into the outlet on the wall. Lights illuminated on the logo of the TV and on the cable box. A small processing fan whirred as it roared to life. The top of the vented cable box warmed.

Girard slid out from behind the TV stand and threw himself toward the sofa. He desperately reached for the remote on the end table. Some of the buttons were elevated like brail on his fingers, and he located the small round one in the center without having to look.

"Come on, come on," he said as the devices powered up slower than they ever had before. He rattled the remote in his hand as though it would help.

No signal.

"Goddammit!"

He tossed the remote on the sofa and rushed back to the TV. He leaned forward and tried to look behind but could not see much. He never did understand this stuff. He hurried back into the kitchen.

Stacey was deliberate in her motions. Her fingertips visibly shook as she struggled to feed the loose phone cord through the bottom of the phone's wall mount.

"Well?" Girard said. The impatience within him begged to wriggle out.

"One sec." The tip of Stacey's tongue stuck out now, sandwiched between her upper and lower teeth.

There was a snap, subtle but noticeable, and Stacey's hands were free. A second phone cord dangled from the wall, which she grabbed and snapped into the bottom of the phone base.

They waited.

Silence.

Seconds turned into minutes. Minutes turned into an eternity. And with each one that passed, Girard felt the hope crumble as nothing happened. His shoulders dipped. His heart sunk. Bernard must have been mistaken.

"What are we doing?" Stacey said. "What's wrong?"

Girard leaned his shoulder against the doorframe, felt the wood flex under the weight of him. "I just thought . . . I don't know what I thought." His head dropped.

"I'm sorry," Stacey said as she walked toward him. "I'm really sorry."

Girard nodded, but that was all he could give.

"I mean it. I know what I did was wrong. And the things I've said to you, they were cruel. I'm sorry."

Girard nodded again. But he looked up when he did and met Stacey's eyes. The glaze was still there and would be for a while, but he felt what she said was genuine, like it came from the heart. And maybe it did.

"Come here," she said. She cautiously raised her arm and rested it around Girard's shoulder. "Let's sit."

Girard relinquished control and followed Stacey's lead. He felt vulnerable, weak, fragile. But it felt good too, to let himself be that way. It was a welcomed role reversal for a few seconds. Trying to be strong all the time was exhausting, and his tank hovered around empty from too many long years of it.

They sat on the sofa. A familiar pressure mounted behind Girard's eyes, but he knew it would not amount to anything. Though he wished this time would be different. A knot in his throat churned and pulsated. He shook his head as nothing happened. Life was the worst.

Stacey got up and walked to the TV, leaned behind it. She fumbled with the cables in the back, then reappeared around the front. In seconds the screen came to life and bright, fully defined features appeared in his living room as if they were there in the flesh. The local newscasters were dolled up in their fancy dress clothes, their faces covered with concealer so their flaws would be hidden from the camera. It was merely a façade designed to fool the people, but not Girard. He was not fooled. He knew the face paint was a guise for the people they wanted the world to see, and the real scars they carried, as people, were buried somewhere deep underneath that. Everyone had wounds. And as Girard observed the man and the woman on the screen try their best to pretend they did not, he wondered what theirs were.

He gave it a minute. Before the commercial break, the woman on the TV teased the top stories they were covering for the day, but none of them were about Miriam. None of them were about the story Bernard said he heard. Girard sighed and flipped the screen to black. He and Stacey sat in the quiet.

Girard did not know Bernard well, but he did not question his character. Some people were trustworthy and some were not, and Girard's instincts told him Bernard was one of the good guys. There would be no reason for him to purposefully deceive. Could it have been a simple case of misunderstanding or misinterpreting or misidentification? It had to have been. He must have been confusing the days or unwittingly mixing up the stories or jumbled the details. Bernard was older than Girard, so maybe he was going senile. It made sense, the possibility of it. Why else would he not have said something before now?

"Do you want to talk about it?" Stacey asked.

Did he? No, probably not. It would only make the situation worse. But if he did not, would Stacey be too concerned to leave him alone, worried about his mental stability? Or would she even care? He could not imagine trying to live another day through his hellish affliction. If for no other reason but to avoid the risk, he needed to convince Stacey he was well so she would go home, and so he ultimately could too.

"It's just that I realized I've been disconnected," Girard said. "And it's probably not a good idea right now."

Stacey looked at him without reacting. She blinked occasionally.

"And before you go, I figured I ought to have you set me back up again. I'll need to make some phone calls this week, take care of some things."

Stacey stayed in character, held her position of nothingness.

"You'll call me, right? When you get home? I can arrange to have your car—"

"Dad?"

"It won't be a big deal. I'll just—"

"Dad?"

Girard sighed. She did not buy it. As it turned out, she was not a complete fool. "What?"

"It's okay. I miss her too."

The knot in Girard's neck twisted again, and this time it pinched away his air.

"I'm really sorry I doubted you. There's just been so much going on, you know? I haven't been in the right frame of mind. I can see how much mom's death is affecting you. There's no way you had anything to do with it."

Girard felt no differently about the situation. While it should have been a relief that Stacey had this realization on her own, nothing seemed to matter anymore. He considered whether now would be an appropriate time to try to talk to her about the green house again—about the waterfall and the frog and the buried urns and the aspirations behind them. It seemed like a prime opportunity to try again, to take one final shot at it. Logically, it made sense. But emotionally, Girard did not have it in him. He could not bear talking about it anymore.

"I need water," he said as he stood. His shirt had dried completely, despite the chaos. He headed for the kitchen.

The glass he filled earlier remained on the counter and served as a reminder of his daily reality. He grabbed the glass, threw his head back, and lathered his throat. The water was not cold, but it still chilled his insides as it swept through his body. He took another swig.

On the way back to the living room, he stopped. His eye caught the illumination on the wall, but he did not believe it at first. He closed his eyes and shook his head, willed himself to stop imagining things that were not real. But when he opened his eyes again, what he saw was not a mirage but instead hope in the form of real-world actuality.

That form?

A blinking red light on the answering machine with the number ten illuminated in the window in the center. Real hope.

CHAPTER TWENTY-EIGHT

Girard knew how dangerous hope was, so he tried to stay as neutral as possible, to remain cautious. False hope was expecting someone to return, even though they were already gone. It was when someone intentionally put on the blinders to ignore the signs and to argue against reality, even though there was no winning. That type of hope could help for a while, to help someone cope with their daily life. But in the end, false hope was just that: false. It could lead to emotional destruction and was bound to end in the ugliest way possible. So one had to be careful.

Unlike false hope, actual hope could provide encouragement and a reason for living, for something to strive toward when life seemed its worst. That type of hope was what drove people to heal in their daily lives. But how did someone identify real, legitimate, healthy hope from false hope? That was the hard part. Sometimes false hope could not be identified right away, and so it was more of something that was morphed into. Having hope meant being emotionally vulnerable, and vulnerability could lead to getting hurt or taken advantage of.

So where did Girard stand? He kept his attention locked on the digits, wondered what those ten messages could be about. They could be nothing—calls from reporters or telemarketers or charities looking for donations. But what if they were meaningful? What if it was just like Bernard said? The messages could be from a hospital somewhere, telling him Miriam was okay. Or they could be from Miriam herself, having left a recording she knew Girard would react to.

But was it false hope or real hope? There was only one way to find out.

"You doing okay in there?" Stacey hollered from the living room.

Was he? It was too soon to tell. He reached for the counter and put the glass down. He feared to let his eyes wander, afraid the number would disappear. Then he moved closer to the answering machine and waited for something to happen, but battled to a stalemate.

"You alright in here?" Stacey said as she appeared in the doorway.

Girard paid her no attention, was instead fixated on the machine. Stacey caught on and followed his gaze, then made her way next to him.

"You expecting a call?" she said.

"No. And certainly not ten."

"You going to listen to them?"

Girard exhaled hard, felt a rush inside him.

This was the decisive moment, was it not? Girard could think of ten potential phone calls—Doctor Brown, the funeral home, the pharmacy, Sergeant Bell; there could easily be ten combinations between them. That was reality. But otherwise, what Bernard said could be true too. He did say the hospital had repeatedly tried to get ahold of Girard—he did use that word, did not he? Girard could not remember. Now he questioned his memory, doubted what had transpired outside. His thoughts sent him into a tailspin.

Girard had the power to end it, to address the doubts, to stop the noise. There was only one way.

He stepped toward the wall. His finger shook as he lifted it—partially from exhaustion, partially from anxiousness—but he had put it off for long enough. One way or another he would get answers. He pressed the crooked triangle button.

The letdown was slow. The bubble he was in was stretched so thin it was in danger of bursting. But rather than that, it leaked instead, a puncture wound the size of the one in his heart sucked the excess air out of the room. The hope fizzled with each press of the button.

Girard was right. The combination of potential callers added up to a lot, and he skipped through them. Sergeant Bell called, twice, to discuss some additional details that came across his desk. This must have been prior to his latest visit. Doctor Brown's office called to confirm his appointment for midweek. Jay from the funeral home called to check in on Girard. That was four.

Girard sensed Stacey deflate next to him, the anticipation in the room all but sucked dry, the hope gone. He considered stopping. He thought about it and seriously weighed it against the alternative. There would still be hope if he left the rest of the messages unheard, but that hope would inevitably get the best of him—and he knew he was not strong enough to handle that. And so he decided he had to know for sure, one way or another, regardless of what the answer may be.

So he did. He pressed on, willed himself to find the strength to push the double arrows that would bring him closer to the truth. What choice did he have?

What happened next changed everything.

The remaining six messages all began the same way: "Hello, this message is for Girard Remington. This is Amy from St. Peter's Hospital. I'm calling about your wife, Miriam."

#

Sergeant Bell and Officer Chatham joined Girard and Stacey in the kitchen, summoned by telephone. They were, understandably, skeptical.

Girard played the six messages repeatedly and listened to every word as if his life depended on it. And in many ways, it did. If this was real, if Miriam was still alive, he would be too.

The dates lined up. The messages began on Friday and ran through the weekend—one each in the morning and afternoon on both Saturday and Sunday. They had already called this morning too. Sergeant Bell was silent, his face as white as the night was dark. Officer Chatham hid behind him.

"Well?" Girard said. "What do you think?"

Stacey moved next to Girard and stood shoulder to shoulder.

Sergeant Bell cleared his throat. "Have you called St. Peter's yet?"

"No. I wanted you to hear this first."

Sergeant Bell nodded. He looked for his partner, motioned, and he ran off. "We'll check it out."

Girard nodded back. He did not know what else to do.

"Listen, if this is true, if your . . . if Miriam is alive, I owe you an apology."

"I don't care about that. I just want my wife back."

A minute passed. It was the longest minute of Girard's life. Each second felt longer than the one before it. When Officer Chatham returned, everyone perked up.

"I spoke with the hospital," he said. "They have your wife."

Stacey wailed and wrapped her arms around Girard's neck as if they were close, though he hardly noticed. His body did not know how to react to any of it.

"Are you sure?" Girard said. "I mean, is she alive?"

"She's fine," Officer Chatham said. A twinge of a smile crept onto his face, his lips parting. "She just wants to come home."

Girard entrusted Stacey's frame with his weight, although not voluntarily. She caught him as his knees buckled, slipped her arms underneath his armpits and held on. It was a mental and physical whirlwind of feels. Through everything, one thing was clear.

Miriam.

With the help of Stacey and the sergeant, Girard steadied himself, found his balance against the wall. The anxiousness moistened his forehead and sucked his eyes dry. He breathed rapidly.

"You good?" the sergeant said. He let go but kept his hands close.

Girard nodded too quickly.

"Take a minute," Sergeant Bell said. "Then we'll give you a ride to St. Peter's."

"I'm coming too," Stacey said.

"No," Girard said, turning toward her. "Later. I need to spend some time with my wife first. Alone."

Stacey was noticeably saddened, a childlike frown formed, but she nodded anyhow. "I'm really sorry about what I did."

"Later," Girard said. "We'll address it later."

CHAPTER TWENTY-NINE

It could happen to anybody once and be a freak thing. But when it happened twice, that meant something. A pattern had begun to develop. And Girard started to question everything he thought he did not believe. First it was the angel of a man who saved him and Miriam from the bitter cold the day after the wreck. That man came and went without as much as a word, forwent a formal introduction and left no way for Girard to contact him to thank him. And now Bernard, their seldom spoken to neighbor who stopped Girard on the street and turned him on to the most improbable life-changing moment imaginable. If it was not for that man, Girard would have emptied the bottle already.

That made twice the universe had sent an angel to save his life.

Could there be another explanation? Girard thought so the first time it happened, though he could not produce one. And now, after it happened again, what could he say? He would need time to process it, though, because everything he thought he ever knew was twisted upside down. He would need time to reflect on his life.

But that would come later. He had plenty of time for that. First came Miriam.

Girard was numb, unable to navigate through the entwined information that invaded his mind. He did not know which question to ask first, or which was most important. If Miriam was still alive, who was in the amaryllis urn in the green house, and what did that mean for Miriam's rebirth in the future? What if he tainted everything by burying the urn too soon?

Rolling hills screamed past the glass as Girard watched through the window. Jagged white lines formed one solid one as Sergeant Bell sped across the pavement, the sirens silent. Route 12 connected the west side of Helena to the east, and smack dab in the middle was St. Peter's Hospital. To think Miriam was so close this whole time was unimaginable, torturous, cruel even. She lay in a hospital bed less than ten minutes from their home, all the while Girard tried to prepare for life without her. None of it made any sense.

A metal grate separated Girard from the two police officers in the front of the cruiser, but he felt free. The demons inside him tried to escape and nearly won. But whatever the forces were behind the green house and the angels on earth kept the demons at bay, and kept Girard from caving into their detestable quest for supremacy. Some things in life would never be explainable by science or medicine or randomization but instead would remain a mystery until it was each person's time to find out. Discovery would happen to each person differently, and their unique path would be their own to experience however they were wired to experience it. Genetics would play a part in how long the journey lasted, as would free will and the effect of the decisions made by each person along their journey. And sometimes luck would play a role, and sometimes it would not always be the good kind.

But one thing was certain, and that was that Girard was glad his journey was still ongoing because he still had so much left to do. He had so much more love to give. And although it took him this long to realize it, he was one of the lucky ones, and he owed it to his creator to live his life to the fullest.

Something happened when the cruiser pulled into the St. Peter's parking lot. Intensity. Girard's focus sharpened, his senses heightened. The seat smelled so leathery Girard could taste it. The wings of the bugs outside the glass buzzed inside Girard's ear. He was aware of the skin on his fingers, how callused it was, how cracked and damaged it felt. Colors were brighter.

Miriam was there. He felt it.

She had a way of doing that to him—making him feel as if he were living outside himself, as if their souls were connected. It was not just the words she seldom spoke, or the careful touch of her fingertips on his skin, or the way their eyes met when the spoken word was not necessary—it was all those things and more. Just her presence heightened Girard's mood and improved his life, and that was not something many people could say about someone else without exaggeration.

With Miriam, he could.

Where did Girard go right to marry this woman? It seemed improbable, unfair to her even, considering the type of man he turned out to be. Miriam deserved so much more, yet she chose him. And she did not regret it. Worse, she loved him back and supported everything he ever did. It was utterly amazing.

The door to Girard's left opened and sunshine spilled inside the back seat. Sergeant Bell stood before him, a little less authoritative than before, resigned to being wrong. Girard admired the man for not letting his ego get in the way of the truth. He owed him a great deal of gratitude for that.

"Are you ready?" Sergeant Bell said. He pulled the door open as wide as it would go.

"Definitely." Girard slid out, incomprehensibly calm. Somehow, his mania stayed out of it—that was Miriam's presence, it had to have been.

"Are you going to be alright?" Sergeant Bell said. "Should we walk on either side of you?"

"I feel great," Girard said. "I've got this."

Sergeant Bell nodded. Officer Chatham smiled. Then the three of them walked toward the sliding doors.

#

They stood outside Miriam's room. Her name was printed on a label and stuck to the outside of a cream folder, which hung on the door. Girard trembled, less controlled.

"You ready for this?" Sergeant Bell said.

Girard took a deep breath but did not respond.

"I'm very sorry."

"Water under the bridge. We're here now."

Sergeant Bell nodded, smiled a little. He reached out his hand, took Girard's, and shook it. "Thank you for understanding."

Girard was a wreck. He was not briefed on Miriam's condition, and so he was not sure what to expect. He should have been there for her from the beginning.

"We'll wait out here," Sergeant Bell said. "But before you go inside, we want you to have something."

"What is it?"

Sergeant Bell motioned to Officer Chatham, who pulled something from his pocket and handed it to his partner. Girard passed his eyes from hand to hand but could not make out what it was.

"Let me see your hand," Sergeant Bell said.

Girard held it out, his fingers spread.

The sergeant dropped something cold in Girard's palm, then forced his fingers closed as he pulled away. He patted Girard's hand and looked at him in the eye and smiled. "You should have this."

Girard clenched his hand, rolled the hard object between the wrinkles on his palm. It had a curvature to it, the circumference that of a small coin or a button, but heavier. The longer he toyed with it, the more familiar it became, but he did not think it could be true. To find out, he opened his fingers and looked down, and a knot in his throat formed.

It was Miriam's wedding ring, charred and all.

"How?" Girard said. "I thought it was evidence?"

"Was. Miriam's alive and well, so the case is closed. The two of you should have it. You need it more than we do."

Girard did not know what to say. The gesture was so gracious there were no words that could do it justice. He stepped toward the sergeant and wrapped his arms around him, breathed in the aftershave that lingered on his neck. He heard the patting on his back before he felt it.

"Thank you, so much," Girard said as he pulled away. "This means the world to me."

"I know it does," the sergeant said, a twinkle of dampness in his eyes. Next to him, Officer Chatham smiled from ear to ear. "Consider it a peace offering."

Girard smiled. "Thank you."

Sergeant Bell blinked fast as his jaw flexed, a feeling Girard envied. "We'll be out here if you need us. Go see your wife."

CHAPTER THIRTY

He saw her before she saw him. Her back was to the door. Girard hesitated, but it only lasted for a second. The woman in the room looked decrepit, slouched in a wheelchair. That was new. But as Girard stepped further into the room, all doubt vanished.

He smelled her. Maybe not the bar of soap she used on her skin or the perfume she occasionally sprayed on her sweaters, but rather the actual scent of her. Of her skin. It made him shiver.

"Miriam," he called out, his voice cracking. He was less than ten feet behind her now, his knees wobbly.

There was no response, which was expected.

Girard stepped closer to her. The handles of the wheelchair stuck out from her shoulders as if they were permanent fixtures. He worried about why she sat in one in the first place.

He reached out slowly so as not to frighten her and rested his hand on her shoulder. The tension in her deltoid jarred him, sent his hand flying backward. Time slowed as Miriam's neck craned toward him, her peppery hair bouncing. Girard stepped around the wheelchair, eager to get a glimpse of his wife from the front.

The first things he saw were the deep abrasions on her cheeks and forehead. Some of them were stitched and covered with butterfly bandages, others were scabbed over with crusted mounds of blood. The bruise on her neck was the color of a rainbow, and her right arm was holstered in a sling in front of her chest.

Miriam's eyes scanned upward, traced Girard's body until their eyes met. When they did, her eyelids burst open. A whooshing sound swept through her nose and throat as she sharply inhaled. Her lower jaw fell as if a hinge had been snapped.

Then she made a noise. It was somewhere between a welp and a wail, and it gurgled in her throat until it exploded in the room. Girard leaped back a full step and reached for the wall. But before he got there, he lunged himself forward and dropped to his knees and grabbed Miriam's frail hands in his own.

Miriam wept like she had held it in for an eternity. Water cascaded down her swollen cheeks and drenched her gown, passed some of it along to Girard in the process. He leaned into her chest and shook. He wrapped his arms around her waist and squeezed, the water on his collar the furthest thing from bothersome. She clutched him back. Her one free hand grabbed a hold of his collar and squeezed until her entire body trembled.

They held each other like that for a while.

When their bodies relaxed and Miriam's sobs faded, Girard pulled away. He found a chair next to the bed and dragged it in front of Miriam, sat it close enough so their knees would touch. Then he lifted his hands and began to communicate the way they had become so accustomed to over the years. It did not require thought anymore.

I cannot believe it is you. I cannot believe you are okay, Girard signed.

Thank God you are here. I was so worried.

You were worried! I thought you were dead. I had a service for you.

Miriam threw her hands over her mouth.

It was everything you said you ever wanted. The urn I picked out is buried in your garden.

Oh, Girard.

Girard reached for Miriam's hands, took them, and brought them to his lips and kissed them. He could not believe he had been given another shot.

But that does not matter, he signed. *You are here now. We will figure all that out.*

Miriam nodded. And she smiled. And she cried.

What happened to you? That is the most important thing. Are you all right?

Miriam leaned back in the wheelchair and sighed. She wiped the tears from her eyes. *I do not know, exactly. It all happened so fast.*

What do you remember? Tell me everything.

Miriam sighed again, but with a smile. Then she told him everything she could remember.

It was fifteen minutes short of ten o'clock. Coffee time. Girard would wrap up in the green house just as Miriam prepared the table, and they would enjoy the silence of the morning together. That was how it went every other day.

Miriam prepared the coffee. She grabbed two mugs from the overhead cabinet and set them aside. The tub of grounds sat in the corner of the counter, the plastic lip discolored from years of daily use. She pulled it toward her and popped the lid, breathed in the smells good and deep.

Something ate at her. It began when she awoke with an urgency she had a tough time ignoring as the day continued. Her God instructed her to follow his commands and deviate from her usual routine, though she could not understand why. At first, she thought she was mistaken. Perhaps it was a lingering dream from the night or a fantasy from the day, but she doubted both as the waking hours passed her by.

With her God, she knew better than to disregard his direction. He had saved her from her darkest days and empowered her to find the strength to redefine herself after her handicap. Some things Girard would never understand, and she accepted that. He was a skeptical man and had every right to be—perhaps in time he would find his way to God, as she had. But that was his choice. Miriam made hers a long time ago. It did not change anything between them.

The urgency with which the silent words were implanted inside her gave her no choice but to listen. And react. They were powerful and would not allow her to ignore them—it was physically painful if she tried, which she did. She had to follow his lead. As guilty as she felt about it, Miriam left everything as it was—the coffee unmade, the mugs unfilled, the container unlidded—Girard would understand. He always did. And though he would be angry with her for taking the Buick, she would ask for forgiveness later and he would give it. God took priority.

One of the chairs in the dining room bit her as she hurried past. It grabbed onto her belt loop and crashed to the floor. The cabinet shook in the corner and the entire floor rattled underneath. Miriam stopped and watched, hoped nothing would fall and shatter. The fallen chair felt as if it were made of granite when Miriam tried to lift it, so she left it. She was in a hurry.

The garage was daunting. The keys shook in her hand as she stood on the step and debated whether she was doing the right thing or not. But the more she deliberated with herself, the clearer it became. Following God's lead was the only right answer.

The garage door made her anxious. Although Girard was preoccupied with caretaking the green house, it had been so long since Miriam had heard the electric garage door open or close, and she was unsure how loud it might be and whether Girard would hear it from the back. So she yanked on the emergency cord and lifted the garage door by hand, then backed the Buick into the driveway. The chains resisted when she tried to pull the door closed once outside, so she pulled it as far as it would go and left it. She would be back before long anyhow, and she would have Girard reattach the chains then. She pulled the Buick into the street and took off in the direction she knew she was supposed to go. For what? She would find out.

Highway 15 brought back memories. Strong ones. Scary ones. Emotional ones. Miriam found herself in tears as she drove it. Driving was like riding a bike for her—although she had not done it in years, since before the accident, it became familiar very quickly. Did she feel confident? No, not exactly. But the volume of vehicles on the road in the middle of the day midweek was low, so she felt adequate.

What bothered her most, aside from worrying Girard, was that she did not have a driver's license. It expired many moons ago without renewal, she never having needed it. She did not know how she would explain it if she were pulled over by the police, so she drove cautiously—she stayed in the right lane, kept a tick or two under the maximum posted speed limit, and always yielded to merging drivers. She would be okay.

She still did not know where she was headed. God's voice had softened inside her, distanced, left her wandering alone on Highway 15 with a major physical disadvantage. Just as the doubt began to creep in, she came upon it. The spot. The scene of the accident. The guardrail that snatched her unborn baby's life.

Miriam flipped her directional to the right and pulled off the road. Tears filled and blurred her eyes. Metal scraped underneath the Buick as it rolled to a stop as she pushed hard against the petal. The vibration of it rolled up her leg. The whole car shook before it came to a complete stop.

Miriam's hands let go of the steering wheel, the whites in her fingers now pink, and went up to her mouth. Tears poured uncontrollably from her eyes, and her chest bounced up and down as she let the sobs overpower her. She spoke words of silence to God, asking him to help her understand what she was doing there, fully aware she would not be able to hear him even if he did speak back. But that was not how God worked, she knew that. The signs would be subtle at best and could pass her by with a simple blink of the eye if she was not careful. But they would be there. If she looked hard enough, she would find what she was looking for, for what God had sent her for.

She opened the door and stepped out of the Buick. A semi breezed past in the fast lane and reminded Miriam of how careful she had to be. She looked twice before she cut across the front of the Buick and made her way toward the guardrail. It had to have been her imagination, but she swore she saw a streak of black rubber on the pavement, which reminded her of one of the last sounds she ever remembered hearing. But that was over thirty years ago, and the roadway had been repaved many times over since then. Sometimes people saw what they wanted to see, regardless of if it was there or not—that was what happened now. That was the miracle of perspective. Or the curse.

Fresh, dark stains lined the pavement underneath the Buick. Miriam leaned down to get a closer look to see if it was from her car but could hardly tell. Surely Girard knew about it if that was the case. The guardrail looked new. The steel bolts had brushed nickel heads and the beam itself still shone with glossy paint. The rail was free of scuffs and dents and rust.

Miriam was not frustrated—she did not feel that way when it came to her God—but she was confused. Flustered, even. She did not understand why she was sent there. There was nothing new to see, the memories she already had. So she decided to head back.

When she turned toward the highway, a scraggy woman stood before her. Miriam's heart leaped and a gasp slid from her lips, but then she smiled and chuckled.

"You scared me," she said.

The woman scrunched her face and twisted her neck, gave Miriam a quizzical look.

"I'm sorry," Miriam said as she pointed to her ears. "I'm deaf."

The woman scowled at her as if she had said something wrong, and Miriam took a step back. The woman screamed at her—she could tell by the reddening of her face and the anger in which she flailed her arms and the general animation of her facial expressions. Miriam knew then she was in danger, though she was awestruck about where the woman came from. Rolling hills surrounded them, and as far as she knew, the only other vehicle that passed by was the semi.

Miriam shot her eyes around, tried to place it all. Behind the Buick was nothing, the same as in the other directions. Miriam figured the woman must have approached on foot. But from where?

The woman was closer now. She uncomfortably invaded Miriam's personal space and made her feel uneasy. Miriam's other senses were heightened since she lost her hearing—she was convinced of it. The ghastly odors her nose captured traveled onto the back of her tongue and slid straight down her throat, and she keeled over and coughed.

The woman's shoes were tattered and different—one used to be white, the other black—and tears covered her sweatpants. Miriam felt terrible for embarrassing the woman who was surely homeless, but it was not intentional. Perhaps all she needed was some help. That, Miriam could offer.

Miriam straightened and looked up. She offered the woman a warm smile, felt the breeze from the morning on her face. But before she had time to react to what would happen next, the woman swung a metal object at her, and everything turned dark.

Girard grabbed onto Miriam's hand and squeezed. His poor Miriam. He did not know what to say to her.

The next thing I knew, I was here. In the hospital. Wearing one of these silly johnnies.

Girard smiled and laughed. He loved Miriam more than anything.

I am so glad you are here.

Girard smiled again. *Me too.* He squeezed her hand harder.

CHAPTER THIRTY-ONE

Girard shared everything that had transpired with Miriam—with the police and the coroner and the exhumation and the news reporter; then about Stacey and Miriam's mini service and the accusations, the brutal, terrible accusations; then he told her about the green house and the burial of the amaryllis urn inside her garden, and about how he had intended to join her later on today; then about Stacey's drinking and his walk in the woods and about Bernard, and the aftermath that followed to lead him to her.

Miriam held him and cried for them, and they clutched on to one another with no intention of ever letting go again.

They sat with each other for hours. Sergeant Bell and Officer Chatham came and went, introduced themselves the best way they knew how, offered their sympathies. Nurses came into the room, along with doctors and hospital management staff. Girard shook more hands than he cared to, was the recipient of more hugs than he felt comfortable with. The number of people who told him how lucky he was, how lucky they both were, made him blush. Most everyone in the room had tears in their eyes, except for him.

The day wound down and he and Miriam both ate. The food tasted nothing like what Miriam would make him at home, but he was thankful to put something in his stomach. And to get a chance to rest. He was exhausted.

Miriam slept. Their hands were linked still, and Girard rubbed his longest finger over Miriam's swollen knuckles. Her raised veins were like dark rivers running underneath her skin. The banks collapsed when Girard pressed them, only to rise again when he let go.

Girard could not sleep. As exhausted as he was, so many thoughts scrambled in his head and made it impossible for him to rest. Miriam's insistence on following God that day made Girard reconsider everything again. Even she was befuddled, it seemed, about why God would send her to that spot on Highway 15 at that moment in time. And when he considered what happened to her, Girard wondered if something else was going on, if maybe Miriam's naivety allowed her to be fooled by the brain invader that challenged her life for so long, like Girard. He worried she was weakening.

Why would God send her? It ate at him to the point of surpassing frustration, dangerously crept toward anger. Why would God do that to Miriam? He sent her and she obeyed, and he repaid her with being beaten nearly to death. And in conjunction—if what Miriam believed was true— testing Girard's strength and willpower to his absolute maximum, only to pull back just enough for Girard to question everything. From what he understood about God, that did not make sense. God was supposed to be the ruler of all that was good in the world, the almighty when it came to loyalty and love and grace. But in his experiences, God was everything but, and that made him angry.

But then he thought about the wreck and the guardian angel that saved them, then about the aftermath and all the horror that followed. And he thought about Bernard and wondered how much of it was a coincidence rather than some larger, superhuman force behind it all. How much of it was even real?

Girard squeezed Miriam's hand again. Her skin felt so good against his own, like he was home, where he belonged. There was a level of comfortability he felt when around her that no other soul, living or dead, could come close to matching. It was more than that even. Miriam put him at ease, made him feel loved, desired, needed. Made him a better person. Life had proven impossible to navigate without her, even for just a few days, and he had never been more thankful for anything in his life than to have her back. His own wishes aside, Miriam's love was all he needed.

Pressure built up behind his eyes. It was the familiar discomfort that made him want to explode inwardly, and sometimes did outwardly. It was his living reminder of all the wrong he had done. But instead of dwelling, Girard looked at his wife—though battered and bruised, she slept peacefully, gently. There were more creases in her skin than there had ever been, and all the kisses from the sun had caused short patches of browning, but she was still the most beautiful woman he had ever seen. And for all the wrong he had done, he did something right with her, and that was all that mattered.

His wife loved him unconditionally, and that was not something every man got the pleasure of experiencing.

Behind him, there was a knock on the door. He turned to peek, then stood up as a middle-aged nurse entered the room.

"Hello, Mr. Remington," she said. "My name's Amy. We spoke on the phone earlier."

Girard accepted her extended hand and shook it.

"I just wanted to come by before I leave for the day, now that everyone else has cleared out." She smiled.

"Thank you for taking care of my Miriam."

Amy dropped a hand on Girard's wrist. It was so soft Girard looked down to see if it was still there.

"It's my absolute pleasure. It's moments like these that make it all worth it."—she smiled again—"How's she doing?"

Girard looked over his shoulder at Miriam and watched her sleep for a few seconds before he turned back. "She's glad I'm here. She seems to be recovering just fine."

Amy nodded, though the smile fell from her face. "Mr. Remington, has anyone told you what happened? Her doctor or another of the nurses?"

"Miriam told me."

She nodded. "Yeah, okay. Yeah, that's good."

"Is there something wrong?"

Amy shot a glance to the hallway behind her, then back to Girard. They were not touching anymore. "I probably shouldn't be telling you this, but I feel a part of it, you know? She's a lovely woman. I find myself getting too attached to my patients these days."—she smiled, but it was sad—"One of the doctors will tell you about it, I'm sure. Probably just waiting for the right time."

"What is it?" Girard's heart pounded hard.

"Your wife was unconscious when she arrived. A state patrolman found her that way and radioed for help. We ran her through a battery of tests when she got here. We didn't know anything about her, not even her name. She had no identification on her."

"Her purse must have been stolen along with the car."

"That's what we figured too. It took time though, once she was awake. She was in and out of consciousness, and we had trouble communicating with her."

"She's deaf."

"Yes, we know now. It took a while."

"Yes, okay, so? You did the best you could. I'm here now."

"No, no. It's not that."

"What then?"

"Did you know . . . Were you aware . . . No, you couldn't have been. There was no way to know."

"What? What is it?"

Amy sighed, looked anxious. "When we ran all those tests—full-body MRI, CT scan, x-rays, blood tests, you name it—we found something."

"Okay."

"It's a miracle in some ways, Mr. Remington. It really is. This never happens. I've never seen it."

"Seen what?"

"On the CT scan, there was a mass on her pancreas. Clear as day. So we biopsied it. And sure thing, cancer."

Girard felt weak.

Amy placed her soft hand on his wrist again. "But that's not the unbelievable part. Pancreatic cancer patients don't typically show any symptoms until it's too late, until the disease has progressed too far. But not here. Unless tested for it on a regular basis, most people never know. And this type of cancer spreads like wildfire. It's often a death sentence."

Girard was dizzy. Amy smiled at him with tears in her eyes as if this was good news, and he did not understand why. His wife, after everything, was still dying.

"Like I said, it's a miracle. It's early, stage one. I've never seen a patient diagnosed with stage one pancreatic cancer without symptoms. Never! The high-risk patients, sure. But not like this. It's an absolute miracle."

Girard was a mess. An utter mess. Nothing made sense. "What are you saying?"

"I'm saying you're a lucky man. And your wife is a lucky woman. As tragic as this incident was for her, it saved her life. The cancer would have eaten her alive."

Girard was physically speechless. He literally had nothing to say, even if he wanted to.

"You two must have done something right because the man upstairs sure is looking after you."

#

As much as he wanted to, Girard did not wake her. She needed to rest. Cancer? Miriam had cancer? She did not deserve that.

An hour passed. Girard was back in the chair in front of Miriam, her tired fingers interlocked with his, her breaths calm and steady. Girard remained anxious. When Miriam finally stirred, her eyes initially became slits before succumbing to the urge to awaken. She blinked away the grogginess and found Girard's eyes, then gave him the biggest, most genuine smile he had ever seen. But it quickly faded.

What is wrong? she signed.

Do you have cancer?

Yes.

When were you going to tell me?

It was too much at one time. I had to give you time to process everything.

I could have handled it.

Miriam smiled. Then she put a shaky hand on his face and rubbed her thumb over the cleft on his lip before retreating. *No, you could not have.*

Girard sighed. She was right. Miriam knew him better than he knew himself. She was so much stronger than he was.

Once the doctor told me that, it all made sense to me.

What did?

Why God sent me.

Explain.

This cancer inside me, it is one of the worst kinds. It does not show any symptoms before it is too late. Usually.

I have been told.

If this never happened, if I had not listened to where God sent me, if I did not get out of the car and reminisce, I never would have known. We never would have known. It would have been too late.

But what about the beating? And the mugging?

God works in mysterious ways, my dear. If only one of those events did not occur in the proper sequence, none of this would have worked out. If I was not beaten unconscious and left without identification, the hospital would not have run all those tests. And without the tests . . .

Yes, I understand.

God is a miracle worker. He can do remarkable things in this world.

Girard leaned back. Information overload. It was an extraordinary sequence of events—there was no denying that. But was it Miriam's God in action, or was life more about interconnected coincidences that altered the events that followed?

*What?*Miriam signed. That wide smile of hers returned, despite the pool of water in her eyes.

Girard leaned closer again, touched the bare skin on her forearm. *It is just . . . The brake lines.*

What about them?

The sergeant told me there was a small puncture in the line. That dark stain you saw on the road, that must have been brake fluid. Miriam, that could have been you. Whoever attacked you and took the Buick, they crashed and burned to death because they could not stop. That should have been you.

Not should. Was not. There is a reason for everything, Girard. If God did not send me out there, it could have been you instead. Or both of us. We would have been in the car together some other day.

Girard nodded, though slowly.

He saved me, but he also saved you too.

I am just struggling with it. Everything that should have happened, that could have happened, almost did. If Bernard had not stopped me on the sidewalk, I would have been lying dead on the floor of the green house by now.

Miriam smiled again, even bigger. *It is called a guardian angel, baby. Sent by God. We have certainly been blessed with more than one of those in our lives, have not we?*

CHAPTER THIRTY-TWO: Monday— Three Months Later

Life was just one big circle of connected events, was it not? Girard had completed the circle. The most impactful seconds of his life, his defining moment, happened on the side of Highway 15 thirty-seven years ago. The universe sent its first angel then, and that was the same spot where it would send his last. The mysteries of the universe would remain unknown.

Angels came in all forms—whether it be a kind but uncredited young man who rescued them from an icy car; the doctors who saved Miriam's life when she was not strong enough to fight on her own afterward; the timid black man from the neighborhood; or the ill-fated Jane Doe who unwittingly sacrificed herself to give them another chance, which led to a sequence of events that could only be described as miraculous.

For Girard, Miriam was his personal guardian angel—he had come to realize that. Her love and her companionship and her understanding—those were wonderful on their own. But the way Girard felt when he was in her presence, the fullness he felt inside, that was rare. Miriam made him a believer in something larger than himself, showed him the way to get there—though to where was still a mystery. Without everything that happened that led up to the next moment they would share together, Girard would not have seen the truth. Miriam was saved to keep Girard on the right track, and by doing so, they would both be able to live out eternity with each other, protected by the powers behind the universe.

Where did the green house fit in to all this? It was clear now. It was influenced by something beyond the physical world, spoken through the language of Girard's personal guardian angel. Girard built it and cared for it and protected it, but the idea behind it—the powers it had, the sensationalism of it—was something bigger. The more Girard cared for it and fed it life and gave it his soul, the more the green house gave back. And with Miriam's encouragement, Girard recognized that and embraced it. Some ideas were bigger than himself.

Mondays held an all new meaning. The sorrow of the weekend still lingered, but the yellow chrysanthemum offered more hope than just for emotional recovery. While Girard lived the last thirty-seven years defined by that dark, frosty night that changed everything, that ended the day he and Miriam were reunited. The weekend sorrow still hovered over them like a cloud ready to burst, but the pain of it hurt less with each passing week. It would never be forgotten. Iris would never be forgotten. But what changed was Girard and his perspective on life.

Terrible things happened to people—good people, bad people, and everyone in between—and that was just how life was. Some of those things were the fault of the person they happened to, some of them were not. Pain and sorrow and regret was everywhere—that was part of the human experience. But there was another side of that too. Hope and happiness and mindfulness—enjoying life's smaller moments as they came, the finest ones—and love. It was okay to feel those things, even after all the bad that happened. It was okay.

Letting go was part of the process—the bad memories and the toxic people and the things one did not care for. Girard was working toward that. He willed himself, with the support of his angel of a wife and the mysterious creator that connected them both, to move on. To forgive himself. He had repented and been forgiven by Miriam, but to forgive himself would take more time. But he would get there.

What happened with Iris was tragic, was one of the ugliest experiences life could throw at him. But it could not define him, would not, not any longer. He would never forget Iris and did not want to, nor would he be able to bottle up the flashbacks that popped up in his dreams even still. But what he could do was move on and love his wife, and maybe one day, himself too. There was hope for that. And for everything else to come—now that he was open to the idea that the end was not really the end, but rather just the beginning.

They still had Stacey in their lives. She had her own issues to tend to, no doubt. And when she addressed those demons and found the resolve within herself to do what she needed to do, Girard would welcome her back into their family. Miriam certainly would too. That was never a question. And that day would come. He and Miriam did not discuss it much because there was nothing they could do.

Stacey checked herself into a facility that would help her conquer the ugly inside her. She would be there for a while. Months, years, who knew? Whatever it took. Girard spoke with her on the phone once each week, and she sounded like she was improving. Though she still had a long way to go. He and Miriam would be waiting for whenever she was ready.

Miriam was on the mend. She was thinner and weaker than she had ever been and was aided by a wheelchair for at least a little while. Maybe forever. It depended on how she bounced back. But her hair was still growing back and the cancer was in remission, and her spirit was as strong as ever. She was a fighter. And a survivor. They both were. The distorted wedding band she wore on a chain around her neck reminded them both of that every day.

When they got home from the hospital, Miriam insisted they walk across the street and thank Bernard together. She figured the man must have been a wreck, doubting whether he made the right decision or not, for he likely never heard how it all concluded. Miriam did not think it was fair that he lived with that burden. She was right, as usual. Bernard broke down in tears when he opened the door, and his wife Jane was there to catch and comfort him, just as Miriam would do for Girard if the roles were reversed. Jane told them they had no idea how badly Bernard needed the reaffirmation from them that he had done the right thing, and so they were both forever grateful. It went both ways. There was no better foundation for a relationship to be built upon.

As it turned out, Jane was an educator in her younger days, like Girard, and she had baseline knowledge of signing. Who knew? So while Girard and Bernard would be forever bonded, Miriam made her first true friend since Rose, outside of her marriage, and she was happier than ever. For Girard, he was still building a relationship with Bernard, but those things took time. The four of them occasionally ate dinner together, rotating from one side of the street to the other, and Girard did not mind. Rather, he enjoyed the company. There was quite a lot they had in common.

Girard still spoke with Doctor Brown on a regular basis. Six weeks into Miriam being home, it was Doctor Brown's opinion that Girard could lessen the amount of medication he took daily, if he wanted to. Though hesitant, he took her advice. The weaning process was slow and steady, but it was ongoing. There were times when his fingertips were numb or when he had blistering migraines or an upset stomach, but that was all part of the process. Miriam was there to support him every step of the way.

He still went to talk therapy sessions with Doctor Brown every week. Though his mindset had changed and his perception was less tranquilized, maintaining a positive mindset was a lifelong effort. And there was no telling what life might have in store for him in the future. He handled things as they came, day by day.

The best part? He could feel again. There were days when he laughed and smiled, and others when he was frustrated and angry—and without the rage. And some days, he would experience all four, and lots of others in between. It had been so long since he felt those feelings that he could not remember if it felt like it used to or not. But this was his new normal, and he was okay with that. He still longed for tears sometimes though.

The emotional highs and lows of life exhausted him—that part he had forgotten about. Too many ups and downs would make him tire easily, but those were the days he appreciated the best. Why? Because they reminded him what feeling alive felt like again, and that was something he was not sure he could ever get back. He thought he lost that. There was so much he was thankful for.

Sergeant Bell and Officer Chatham did not come around again after they left the hospital. The sergeant called once to talk about Jane Doe from the accident, but there was not much to say. Nobody had been reported missing that fit her general description—or what was known of it, which was not much—and nobody had called asking about her. She was a mystery and would remain that way forever. Especially since there was no body to extract DNA from anymore. Some people just vanished off the living earth without a trace—she was one of them. Wherever she was meant to go, she would be there by now. Girard knew that. And as strange as it may be, considering what she did to Miriam, Girard was grateful for her. Life would have been vastly different without her, and not in a positive way.

Beyond that, Sergeant Bell and Officer Chatham were strangers now, and that felt appropriate. Ultimately, they had jobs to do and did them, and their efforts were done. On to the next. Girard supposed that was how it was intended to be. Perhaps their paths would cross again one day, or maybe not. Only time would tell.

One question lingered when Girard brought Miriam home. What to do with Jane Doe's ashes? What was right? She attacked Miriam unconscious, stole her purse and her jewelry and the Buick, and got burned to a crisp on the side of Highway 15 when the brake line gave out. But she also saved Miriam's life, which in turn saved Girard's, which, perhaps, would save Stacey's. She deserved something, did not she? But, what? They sat on the answer to that question for months. Three of them.

#

What if we leave her? Miriam signed after getting Girard's attention. He clipped the weeds in the garden while she watched.

Girard put down the clippers and walked over to Miriam. *Jane Doe?*

Yes. What if we leave her?

But that is your garden. That is what you always wanted.

And I can still have it.

What are you thinking?

I owe her life. As nasty as she may have been to me, she did not deserve to die. I deserve to give her another chance at revival.

What are you suggesting?

There is room for both of us. Do you agree?

Well, yes. I suppose so.

Then that is what I want. I do not want to disturb her. You can dig another hole for me, right?

Of course.

Then it is settled. Let us give her a chance to blossom.

Okay. Then we shall.

About the hole?

Yes?

You can make it large enough for both of us, right? For you and me and her, I mean.

Girard smiled. *Of course. If that is what you want.*

It is. I want you with me. I need you with me. In life and after it.

A kaleidoscope of butterflies fluttered in Girard's abdomen. Oh, how he missed those.

I love you, Miriam signed.

I love you too. With all my heart.

#

They went for a ride. The insurance company paid up and arranged for a replacement for the Buick. They chose another one, black this time. For Iris. Miriam was buckled in tight, an anxious hand held on to Girard's wrist as he took the corner slowly. He knew they had to face their fear sooner rather than later if they wanted to conquer it. And so together, they would.

He seldom did this because of the guilt, but something told him to today. As he drove, he craved music, longed for the sound of someone's voice besides his own. Miriam shifted her eyes at him when he pushed his finger toward the radio. She smiled and signed that it was all right, and that was exactly what he needed—her approval.

The radio flipped on. The volume was low, but it was plenty loud enough. The new Buick did not rattle as the old one had, and so the only sound otherwise was that of tiny pebbles being tossed away from the spinning rubber. He found a country western station and left it there, took in the harmonious rhythms of the banjos and harmonicas and acoustic guitars. He did not hear many of the words, just the music. It was an extraordinarily pleasurable experience. Pure serenity.

Before long, Girard pulled the Buick into the cemetery. They were the only vehicle in the lot. Iris's headstone could be seen from a distance, a paved labyrinth before it. The afternoon was pleasant and the sun shone, and Girard had his sneakers on. He unpacked Miriam's wheelchair from the trunk and unfolded it, then wheeled it next to Miriam's door. He helped her into it while he kept it steady, the leather handle soft and smooth. When she was settled, he locked the car and held on tight, and they started for Iris's headstone.

The grass that surrounded it was recently mowed, but the stone looked lonely by itself. Girard took the flowers Miriam picked from the garden and arranged them in front of the headstone, laid the stems down first, and let the petals fall with grace as if they were feather pillows.

There were just two of them. One was a bearded black iris before the storm. The reason was simple: it was Iris and what represented her; it was how they would always remember her. The other flower was a yellow chrysanthemum—it was Monday, after all. But more than that, it was what the flower represented in their world—the hope. There was always hope for Iris, and for them. Always.

Girard wrapped the two stems together and stepped back so they could enjoy. The scenery was beautiful. Pinks and reds and blues and whites were everywhere, but no blacks, not until now. The one black stood out among the others, which was fitting. Iris would have been a one of a kind, and she deserved the attention.

They headed back. Miriam held her left arm above her head and rested it on Girard's hands on the handle of the chair as he pushed. Her warmth made him want to melt. When Miriam was strapped back in the Buick and her chair was folded up and secured in the trunk, Girard climbed in the driver's seat. The new engine started up like it was nothing and roared to life under Girard's feet.

Then he heard it.

He froze.

Miriam nudged him to grab his attention, then put a hand on his face and pulled it toward her so she could see his eyes. Everything was blurry.

What is it? Miriam signed.

Girard did not know what to say. It could not be happening. It seemed there were surprises everywhere he turned these days.

What is it, darling?

He wished he could explain it to her. He wished he knew how to say it.

Girard, you are crying.

And he was. He did not realize it. He sat up straight and peeked in the rearview and saw it for himself. Both eyes were filled with water, and a tear threatened to roll off his eyelids. He watched in amazement.

How about that? he signed. *I am crying.*

My goodness. Miriam turned his head toward her again and wiped his tear with her finger. Then she pulled him close and kissed him ever so softly on the lips.

The song, he signed. *It is playing.*

Miriam smiled. *Of course it is. Like I have told you, God works in mysterious ways.*

Girard smiled back at her. They would never completely agree about the origin of the mysteries of the universe, but he had to admit his curiosity. He felt his heart sprint under his skin at the thought of the unknown.

He buckled himself in and held on to Miriam's hand while he turned the Buick around and headed for the road. Miriam pulled his hand to her lips and kissed it, and he did the same to hers. They traded smiles. And as the open road became theirs as Girard drove toward home and for the green house where he belonged, Conway Twitty wrapped up his song and signed off.

What a shame, what a sight. A good love died tonight.

THE END

AUTHOR'S NOTE

Dear Reader,

Thank you for choosing to spend your time with me. How was it? This book is deeply personal to me, and I am happy to share it with you. I would love to hear your thoughts. Feel free to shout-out on Instagram or Facebook or Twitter, or to reach out via email. You can find my information on my website: www.danlawtonfiction.com.

If you would consider sharing a few sentences about your experience with the book anywhere you love to talk about books, I would be grateful. In the meantime, happy reading!

All the best,

Dan Lawton

ABOUT THE AUTHOR

Dan Lawton is an award-winning literary suspense, mystery, and thriller author from New Hampshire. He is an active member of the International Thriller Writers (ITW) Organization.

Dan's fourth novel, Plum Springs, won the 2019 New Hampshire Writers' Project Readers' Choice Award for Fiction. His first novel, Deception, was named one of the best thriller novels of 2017 by the Novel Writing Festival. Visit danlawtonfiction.com for all the ways to connect.

Facebook – www.facebook.com/danlawtonfiction
Twitter – https://twitter.com/danlawtonauthor
Instagram – https://www.instagram.com/danlawtonauthor/
Website/Blog – www.danlawtonfiction.com

Thank you so much for reading one of our **Literary Fiction** novels.

If you enjoyed our book, please check out our recommended title for your next great read!

The Five Wishes of Mr. Murray McBride by Joe Siple

2018 Maxy Award "Book of the Year"

"A sweet...tale of human connection...will feel familiar to fans of Hallmark movies." –*KIRKUS REVIEWS*

"An emotional story that will leave readers meditating on the life-saving magic of kindness." –*Indie Reader*

View other Black Rose Writing titles at
www.blackrosewriting.com/books and use promo code
PRINT to receive a **20% discount** when purchasing.